Will NoSky

Fatal Delivery

Privateer Captain Jennifer Bane novels:

FORCED DELIVERY (#1)

Privateer Captain Jennifer Bane won't let the death of a little girl stand. But her enemies can read minds.

After brokering a truce in a war she never wanted to be a part of, Jennifer learns that children are dying because the medicine they need is being hijacked en route. Then Jennifer discovers that people are remarkably reversing their ages on her home planet of Markem just as democracy is finally taking hold.

Are the hijackings and reverse aging a plot by the opposition party on Markem to destroy democracy? Or is there a new alien race responsible? There were rumors about telepaths that could kill with thought, but Jennifer had never gone up against them before—until now.

Can Jennifer deliver the impossible: punish those responsible and save democracy on Markem?

FRAGILE DELIVERY (#2)

When Privateer Captain Jennifer Bane's fiancé is kidnapped, she is injured and unable to rescue him alone. Accustomed to being the lone apex predator, Jennifer has to let the people that care about her find him. With the help of her two sworn vassals, and the two women she rescued from a defiled life of slavery, they join forces. It's pack predation this time, the best way to hunt what you're trying to catch.

No longer about finding one man, it's a race to end the cruelty created by beings without morals. To stop genetics for profit. To destroy a resort that's hunting beings for sport.

RETURN DELIVERY (#3)

Privateer Captain Jennifer Bane is finally about to wed Station Director Krachy...Or is she? Plans take a turn when the day before she is framed for murder and attempted kidnapping during a riot.

The mayhem starts because citizens are outraged that the serial killers on Biltmire Space Station have not yet been captured. Now Jennifer must prove her innocence while being pursued by deranged sociopaths wielding a lethal new weapon.

Unfortunately for the killers, Jennifer and her wedding party refuse to back down—good thing because the maniacs intend to take over the entire space station!

If Jennifer stops them, she may be able to find a way to get married…

FATAL DELIVERY (#4)

ONE

Jeffrey Jansen was jerked awake in his rack by the touch on his arm in the night. Before his sleep-blurred gray eyes focused on the woman leaning down over him, a hand covered his mouth.

"I'm here, Vassal Jansen," came a soft whisper. "You needed me and here I am. Just like how you've been there for me." The thin young woman removed her hand.

Jeffrey Jansen had sworn fealty to Jennifer Bane years earlier to become her vassal. His Lord Bane's voice soothed him, allowing his initial alarm to retreat into insignificance. Their ongoing kinship tie was genetically irreversible. Jeffrey lived to serve and bring honor to his lord, but in this instance he needed her help, not the other way around. Actually, the entire planet of Beltina needed her help, but Jennifer was not aware of that. She only knew her vassal had asked her to come.

He was not the least bit upset his unrestful sleep had been broken by her; if anything he was ashamed.

"—I, I, just couldn't make it to your wedding, my Lord," Jeffrey stammered rising on his elbows.

Jennifer eased herself down onto the side of his rack searching his face.

"I got married after I was arrested and thrown into Biltmire Detention. How could you have been there for that?" She assured him, her eyes refusing to show blame.

Jennifer had been on Biltmire Space Station five months earlier when she got married. Jennifer and her husband had helped put a stop to an uprising on the space station with the help of her wedding party. She was incarcerated at the time of their marriage. A strange twist of circumstances for sure. After the wedding in detention, the charges against her were dropped.

The star-lit depths of deep space were serene beyond the viewport in Jeffrey's command cabin aboard the Receiver Communication Station. He was the commanding officer. Beltina's technological marvel was capable of transporting spaceships instantaneously through hyperspace. The Receiver was built to use incredibly compressed molecular energy to power the Nano Disassembler Manipulation Process for use in the transmission radio wave. An object would be disassembled via the NDMP then reassembled during the Nano Reassembler Manipulation Process. Once reassembled, the object would arrive in the receiving cage of the Receiver blinking back into existence after traveling through hyperspace. The receiving cage was a large communication dish built into one side of the enormous rectangular space station.

Ever since the troubles on the planet Beltina had begun, Jeffrey had felt no safety. The prime minister of Beltina was too hesitant to impose martial law on the planet with so much distrust. There was a reason for the distrust—a big reason.

Jennifer stood as Jeffrey swung his legs over his rack looking up at her.

"The abductions on Beltina are getting worse." That was the big reason. Jeffrey closed his eyes to the thought, not wanting to picture more lives disrupted and families destroyed. He looked up at his liege lord, but her face remained an impassive mask. However, her green eyes were icy. What little information Jennifer knew about the abductions filled her with anger.

Jennifer waited.

Jeffrey stood up as Jennifer backed away a few paces. He was six-feet-four but didn't tower over her; she was six-feet tall herself. She carried herself with conviction and aggressive pride. Her stature and poise were evident under her slim-fit black crew neck long-sleeved shirt and blue trousers. Her sandy brown bob haircut framed her thin face.

Scratching noises on the ceiling pulled Jeffrey's eyes up. Perched upside-down were two tan insect-like creatures. Their three-and-a-half-foot-long bodies wore a piece of vest-like clothing around their abdomens holstering a laser pistol each. Two sets of legs extended from their thoraxes and another set from their abdomens. Their thorax tilted upward keeping the creature's head angled up as they moved.

"They act as bodyguards when I need them, Jeff," Jennifer explained as Jeffrey grabbed his trousers pulling them on over his shorts.

"You met them before when they helped us infiltrate the hunting resort to rescue Krachy and their friends," she continued, referring to her husband Krachilavito Bantor and the Insect Aliens (IAs for short) that were a part of Krachy's small team being hunted like prey by idiot amateur safari seekers. Jeffrey and Jennifer, along with a sizable team, had rescued Krachy and two IAs who were a part of Krachy's team from the resort. The two IAs on Karachy's team were friends with the IAs above.

Jennifer realized Jeffrey didn't fully understand and answered the puzzled look on his face.

"After I got married in detention, then was released, they showed up on Biltmire Space Station. They flashed a picture of Krachy to Station Security and he did the rest. Since he's space station director he allowed the two IAs on-station. When Krachy and I went to meet them, they did their circle dance thing around me several times. That's their way of communicating to each other and to me. So now, they step in to cover my back when I need them. I figured out early on why they gravitated toward me." Jeffrey stopped pulling on his low boots waiting for her to continue.

"Since they can read minds, they knew I'd been suffering from cumulative head trauma and concussions. They came to protect me, and my head, as a way of thanking me for rescuing their friends off the hunting resort. They must have pitched their minds across space and read my mind—my condition. Whenever Dimitri is not around they help protect me," she explained referring to her other sworn vassal Dimitri Volodya.

Jeffrey slipped on his low boots, then finished dressing in his dark blue tunic stepping toward the exit hatch. He ran his hands through his red hair smoothing it. Instead of addressing Jennifer he looked up at the two IAs.

"Thank you for looking out for my Lord."

The two IAs made no acknowledgement, emotion not an instinctual part of their race. All they did was cast their two sets of compound eyes on Jeffrey.

Jeffrey started to go down on one knee as a sign of traditional honor-bound submission before his lord, but Jennifer stopped him grabbing his arm.

"No, Jeff. Not this time. You don't have to do that. I came here for you. As many times as you've covered my back, and saved my life, I'm honored to help you now."

Jeffrey was overwhelmed that his lord would do this for him. The concept of a liege lord honoring and serving her vassal was not commonplace. But then most everything his liege lord got involved in was not commonplace—far from it.

Jennifer saw his confusion.

"Don't fight it, Jeff," Jennifer advised. "I have access to resources that you don't. My ship parked orbit not far from here. I traveled to the Receiver in a cargo shuttle from Food Theory Commodity Station. Carol Bouquet, a good friend I met before my wedding, is posing as a sales rep from Food Theory on a fake sales cold call to see if she can drum up some business from you. That was my cover to come aboard."

Jennifer reached up touching the sub-vocal mic on her throat.

"I even keep in contact with Carol via this."

Jeffrey cleared his throat.

"The prime minister of Beltina would like to speak with you."

Jennifer's eyes were cold as a winter sky. She tensed noticeably.

"The abductions," she stated neutrally.

"No, not that."

Jennifer's face paled, afraid of the real reason.

Jeffrey's eyes narrowed then shot a concerned look at the IAs on the ceiling before returning his weighty stare to Jennifer.

"It has to do with them actually," he jabbed a thumb heavenward toward her two bodyguards. "Their entire race, I mean. The prime minister wants you to act as a go-between in an attempt to integrate the Insect Alien Collective into Beltan society. Lad Blanconales asked for you specifically. He would like you to be the IA Ambassador. He knows about your familiarity with their race."

A slice of adrenaline knifed Jennifer's chest but it didn't register on her face.

Jeffrey knew asking this would upset her.

Beltina was the first planet to learn about the Insect Aliens. Jennifer was the person that provided the proof. What Jennifer had discovered about the IAs since that time was that they had a rebellious splinter faction. These rebels did not want to follow the direction of their main leaders called the *Collective*.

Jennifer remained silent, green eyes unreadable.

Jeffrey felt terrible asking this of his lord but was obligated nonetheless. Jennifer long ago decided that she did not want Jeff supplanting his life to follow her around privateering. Jennifer had been a privateer up until about three years ago when the stress of the mission she was on caused her to quit. Now, at age 34, she was easing herself back into that difficult profession. She'd promised herself not to take on missions that would be a detriment to her health or the health of others. And to not put her life on the line leaving her new husband a widower.

5

Jennifer's health was tenuous to say the least. She suffered from cumulative head trauma, with the last serious incident bordering on a traumatic brain injury. She had a vial of prescription meds in her pocket for the condition that she unconsciously rested her hand over now. The medication helped control her symptoms—they were a crutch she could not live without.

Trouble always seemed to chase her. The chronic head trauma she was now living with forced her to be hyper-sensitive about *anything* that would add to her decline—like being asked to be an ambassador to the Insect Alien Collective, which she knew for a fact, had a rogue group of individuals with independent thought and dark ulterior motives. The reason Lad Blanconales wanted her for the job was precisely because she *did* know this and had seen it all firsthand—too firsthand, unfortunately.

Jennifer clinched her jaw fighting a rising panic.

"No, no way, Jeff!" This was beyond what she was physically capable of handling. It frightened her to the core just talking about it. She had come here determined to help Jeffrey, but this was too much!

Jennifer turned fast. Jeffrey failed to grab her arm as she rifled a hand past the scan pad next to the exit hatch opening it. She sprang out into the long corridor as if running for cover.

The next set of things happened in blisteringly quick progression.

Jennifer's eyes focused on a small floater drone closing the distance toward her down the corridor.

One of the Insect Aliens darted out the hatch behind her backward with all six legs trailing its lunging body.

The other IA thrust itself through the hatch with blinding speed landing on Jennifer's right shoulder and pushed off hard.

The shove propelled Jennifer left, out of the path of the oncoming floater, into the waiting legs of the IA that had landed with its back against the corridor wall. Two of the legs softly, somehow, cradled her head, the other four her body.

The IA on the right pushed off the other wall landing on the deck in front of Jennifer as Jeffrey dove atop her back creating a sandwich with Jennifer in the middle. The IA caught Jennifer and Jeffrey cushioning them from hard impact. The immensity of the strength it took was not reasonable.

The left IA pushed off the corridor wall in a blur, using its six legs to push the floater through the open hatch behind them as it exploded.

Jeffrey shielded Jennifer from the oncoming blast.

Jennifer cut loose with a loud screech from deep in her chest an instant before the corridor's atmosphere split apart in a peal of catastrophic noise. The scream saved her eardrums from the effect of the blast.

The deafening shockwave boiled violently out through the hatch and over the back of Jeffrey's legs, butt, and back shearing off his clothes—along with at least two layers of skin. The savage cough of concussive force singed the raw skin underneath blood red. Jeff's prone body protected Jennifer from the blazing heat of the boomer's shockwave.

Jeffrey was awake as his head turned seeing Jennifer's left hand for a brief instant. He smiled inwardly spotting the modest gold wedding band on Jennifer's ring finger before he blacked out due to the intense pain.

Jennifer took a few seconds to determine that she was still alive. She opened and closed her mouth trying to force the high-pitched ringing in her ears to subside.

The IA under Jennifer remained still, holding the weight of her and Jeffrey's limp body with an ease not seemingly possible for a creature as small as it was.

Jennifer stretched her jaw side-to-side blinking rapidly pulling sound back into her ears.

The concerned face of Carol Bouquet looked down at her as she came to a rushing halt. Jennifer was face down and couldn't see her.

"You okay!?" She yelled.

Jennifer pulled in several gulps of air when the burnt flesh smell from Jeffrey's backside registered in her nostrils. Her eyes exploded open but she didn't move, afraid that if she did, she'd add to his injuries.

"Get help!" Jennifer yelped, her throat constricted in fear.

"On the way…" Carol reassured her, talking into her hand comp. She went down on one knee careful not to touch Jeffrey. It looked like the IA underneath them had things stable and safeguarded.

"Jeff! You okay!? Jennifer cried out. "Jeff!"

Carol did what she could to reassure her.

"He passed out, Jen. Help just arrived."

Carol pushed herself standing. She backed up a few paces as one of the two medicos who had just arrived began fastening a head immobilizer around Jeffrey's neck. The younger man gently looped his hands under each ankle to steady the patient. Once Jeff's neck was cinched in the immobilizer, the young guy at Jeffrey's feet grabbed the scoop stretcher from atop a gurney they had brought with them.

"You're going to have to help me. Get down here," the young medico instructed Carol as he looked up.

Carol did as she was told. She watched the medico pull the scoop stretcher apart splitting it vertically into two parts. He handed one of the shaped blades towards Carol which she grabbed, then figured out what the man wanted her to do. The man pushed the blade he was holding under Jeffrey's chest with practiced ease. Carol pushed her blade under his chest and legs until the two halves were brought together underneath. The securing clips at the top and bottom both engaged with an audible *click*. All the while, the older medico cradled Jeffrey's neck in the immobilizer just to be sure, then quickly switched on the anti-grav unit on the scoop stretcher.

The scoop stretcher lifted Jeffrey off of Jennifer. The older medico guided Jeffrey's prone body onto the gurney, activated the anti-grav unit on the gurney, then quickly guided him down the corridor.

The younger medico stood looking down at Jennifer.

"Are you injured?"

Jennifer was clearheaded enough now to focus on the small IA underneath her. The two unblinking red-hue colored compound eyes of the alien were unflinching as was its six legs positioned under her strategically, balancing her, with a gentleness that was not from this world.

"I'm okay, just some ringing ears." Jennifer gulped back tears realizing this creature, his friend, and Jeffrey had just been willing to sacrifice their lives to protect her.

The medico hearing the distress in her voice, thought she was getting sick.

"You sure?" The man went down beside her in a push-up turning his head sideways to look into her watery eyes.

Jennifer nodded screwing her eyes shut, a few tears dropping to the deck past the head of the IA. She opened them.

"Yeah, yeah, I'm fine. Just help me up."

The man was already grabbing her waist and pulled her standing so fast that Jennifer wobbled when both feet connected with the deck. Steadied, she wiped her eyes with the back of a hand watching the IA spring up and scale the wall beside her to reunite with its friend on the ceiling. The two IAs did their circle dance around each other quickly.

The young medico nodded gravely at Jennifer, then jogged down the corridor. The older medico guiding the anti-grav gurney had already turned the corner at the far end of the corridor out of sight.

Carol was about five-three with a blonde crown topping her pixie bob haircut. She shot her hands to her waist and twisted one side of her face. Her haughty look pinned Jennifer.

"I'm fine, thank you very much!"

Jennifer's face began to turn red with anger not liking Carol's piss-poor timing with the attitude.

"What?! You think I don't care what happened to Jeffrey?" Carol scoffed. "He was breathing when he left here, Jennifer.

It's safe to say that whoever just tried to kill you knows you're here and why. Don't you think?"

Jennifer was starting to regret letting Carol listen in on her conversation with Jeffrey earlier. The look on Jennifer's face nearly peeled the skin off Carol's cheeks.

However, Carol was strong-willed herself, and older than Jennifer. She didn't wither one bit under Jennifer's leer. She just kept trying to get through to her.

"Your two IA friends are okay. Jeffrey's going to be okay. They just saved your life. All of them, together, as a team. Just be glad the three of them were so fast."

"I effin' hate when you big sister me!" Jennifer huffed.

"You're acting like a ruddy child when you should be grateful. *I'm* grateful."

Carol glanced up appreciatively at the IAs.

"Thank you, guys! Maybe Jennifer will make the right decision after all this and actually volunteer to make a difference. What'd ya think?"

The two Insect Aliens crawled down the wall in a blur. They slowed in front of Jennifer as she looked down at them.

The two IAs were motionless staring up at Jennifer with unblinking eyes.

Slowly, they did a few circles around each other and stopped, then cast their eyes up at Jennifer again. They agreed it seemed.

Jennifer's breathing began to slow, and a more natural skin color returned to her face. Some of her anger about what just happened, and Carol's way of looking at things, escaped loudly through parted lips pushing a lung full of air with it.

"You gripe my butt sometimes, Carol. Especially when you're right."

Jennifer looked at the IAs, "Thank you." She dipped her head gratefully.

The IAs were very still, placid.

Jennifer was more than used to this type of behavior from her friends. She had seen it so many times it was pedestrian.

Carol saw the revelation form behind Jennifer's eyes at the thought.

"See what I mean? You know these creatures better than anyone. Go see what the prime minister wants."

Jennifer shot a hard look at Carol. She did not like having her mind read by a human.

Carol tried to reason with her.

"Do you want to take some cover now? I think your team has had enough excitement for one day, don't you?"

Jennifer's frown loosened a bit acquiescing, albeit grudgingly.

"Yes. The last thing I want is for anyone else to get hurt on account of me."

TWO

Jennifer pounded a hard fist into the table next to the recessed keyboard in the conference room just off the bridge of her ship *Viper II*. She cradled her aching hand in her lap. The blow had done most of its job, releasing some of her fury about what had happened to Jeffrey.

Her head came up staring at the now blank screen on the bulkhead that just moments before had held the injured face of her sworn vassal.

A knock came at the hatch.

"Enter!" Jennifer snapped loudly.

First Officer Ian McKivey stood in the hatch frame. He was just over six-foot-six in height, with wide shoulders disappearing down into a slender waist, his torso lean, blonde hair and blue eyes, eyes that were tentative but unwavering. He was as close a friend as Jennifer had ever had. He was the first recruit she had ever enlisted when she struck out solo as a privateer.

"What do *you* want?" Jennifer growled, directing her anger at Ian even though completely unwarranted.

Ian remained calm, watching her.

Jennifer breathed out exasperated.

"I'm a curse to everyone around me."

Ian pulled his lips into a thin line.

"Stop that!" Jennifer hissed, then more softly. "Please…"

"What do you want to do, Jennifer?"

Jennifer had formed an answer, but her answer would protect the many and expose the one.

"You wanna go back home and see Krachy? I'll take you there, no problem."

Krachy was the *one*.

Despite what she had already decided, or perhaps because of it, Jennifer shut her eyes. She pictured Krachy, but his image was quickly dislocated. It was replaced by Jeffrey's face on screen moments earlier looking down at the vid cam below the mobility bed he was lying prone in. He was face down looking through the opening framing his face. The nurse in the ICU section of Receiver Medico had placed the vid cam on the floor so that Jennifer could speak with him briefly.

Jennifer scanned Ian's face.

"The only thing I know right now is that I left Jeffrey without even apologizing."

"Did you just apologize to him on that tight beam vid trans?"

Jennifer clinched her jaw. Ian could almost hear her molars grate.

He knew the answer.

"Then let it go, Jennifer. It's in the past. Just be glad he's alive. And so are you. If you'd gone to visit him it may have given another set up team a chance to finish what they started. You did the right thing."

Jennifer's forehead ribbed.

"Are you mad at me, Ian? I mean secretly. You'd tell me if you were, wouldn't you? You have to be mad that I carry around a hex with me."

"If Carol were here she'd get on to you for feeling this profoundly sorry for yourself. I won't do that though. You know what my response to your question is, don't you?"

Jennifer swallowed.

"How can you put up with me when I harm people that I care about like this?"

No answer was needed. Ian knew it and Jennifer did too.

He moved to her side as she stood and wrapped her arms around his neck burying her head in his chest.

After a few moments she pulled back resting her hands on his big biceps. Her looked changed, no longer sorrowful.

"I know what I want to do."

***

On a healthy slice of blind faith, Jennifer started out. She had chosen to be alone. Even as obsessed as she was about protecting her own health, she knew it was safer for everyone around her to do this by herself. The only person, or being, that could be harmed if something happened to her was her husband. He was the *one* that would endure the full weight of her actions. She was too much of a coward to contact him and look him in the eye to tell him. Krachy was the only man she had ever known that could make her falter in this way. So Jennifer made Ian do it for her.

Hell, with as bad as she was feeling after leaving Jeffrey to suffer his injuries alone, what would it matter to add one more guilt trip to the tally? She could not bring herself to tell Krachy that she was going to break her promise to him. A promise not to take on a mission that she knew would be a detriment to her health.

That mission was not to be an ambassador. The mission was to find out who tried to kill her and injured Jeffrey instead.

Jennifer wasn't naive enough to think that the truth behind it all would be unproblematic. Seeking revenge was fine as far as motivations went. It was just that vengeance never had blinders attached to it. Almost being killed for something that Jennifer hadn't even done would lead to wide-ranging implications. A planet wanted to assimilate a new race into their population. Some groups would want this, others would not. The only way to survive the clash between many competing forces was to travel within that labyrinth deftly. Jennifer would have to pick and choose which passageway provided the most benefit and avoid the labyrinths lacking true value add. Yes there would be noise, enticing options for distraction. Jennifer understood this. The only real question was could the path she'd chosen be traveled alone? No, not entirely. Yes, to a calculating and streetwise extent.

Jennifer being solo did not mean, however, that she did not have the backing of a significant amount of resources. Resources of all manner, type, and race.

Jennifer's Chief Security Officer Linden Kay had served under for a long time when she was the captain of *Viper II*. He was there when she brokered a truce between her home planet Markem and Beltina. Linden had always impressed Jennifer with his professionalism. That professionalism and unyielding determination came up with her first lead.

Jennifer looked at the flechette rifle on the rooftop next to her. The sleek weapon was fitted with an auto sniper scope and muffler to deaden the muzzle sound. It was chambered for 7mm darts. But right now she had no real intention of using it when the person that she had under surveillance came home. It was beside her for self defense only at this point. She wanted to talk with the woman that lived in the building across the street. A woman made wealthy by the blood of good people. The blood of Jeffrey Jansen. The woman had sold the floater drone that tried to kill Jennifer but had injured Jeffrey instead.

Jennifer was using her hand comp now, which in turn, was piped into the attack shuttle she had used to break orbit and land dirt-side on the planet Beltina. She had landed on the outskirts of the mid-sized city of Sommerville and docked her small ship in the city's only space port. Her HC was connected to the tight beam vid comm repeater on her shuttle. This allowed Jennifer to talk off-world to Linden who was still aboard her ship *Viper II* in orbit.

"She just landed at Sommerville's space port," Linden advised. "She has an air car parked there that she should be using for her trip home. I haven't been able to make a dent in, or otherwise hack, her home cyber system. She's put as much work into securing her home that you're watching as she does selling floater drones armed with explosives. Since there aren't many people that deal in her trade, she was easy to pinpoint."

"Did your attempted intrusion on her home systems trip any of her electronic security, Linden?" Jennifer asked.

For Linden to be caught off guard by such measures was more circumstantial evidence that Laura Measures was a woman with quite a bit to hide.

"Yes, she is using some truly impressive artificial intelligence security."

With the woman's homecoming imminent, Jennifer cut the feed and abandoned her sniper hide on the roof, making her way to the back alley behind the building. A quick trip to the rental air car, and the rifle was safely stashed in the boot out of site.

As she made her way across the street, concealed on her person was a laser pistol and a familiar laser blade knife. She carried them in the bum bag around her waist along with several other crucial items that had proved invaluable in protecting her health in the past.

Jennifer decided to use one of the public lift tubes in Laura Measures' building. She had another method of getting up to the woman's flat seven stories above but decided against using it. Linden mentioned that Measures had outfitted her domicile with some impressive AI security. Therefore trying to gain access to the woman's apartment from the outside would not work. This ingress would have to be done the old fashion way—from inside the building.

Jennifer rode the lift tube as far as the floor beneath Measures'. The top floor was only accessible via a private lift tube that Jennifer couldn't gain access to without a secure key card. Linden had tried to hack the system, but AI countermeasures stonewalled the security tech. With Measures' homecoming just minutes away, Jennifer would have to make do with more primeval means. When the lift tube stopped, she climbed up on the handrail, punched through the access hatch above with the hand that wasn't aching, and clambered through.

Jennifer wore a simple pair of blue trousers and a black long sleeved top. She reached in the left pocket pulling the fabric inside-out. A quick grab into the bum bag for the laser blade, she snapped it on, the low hum of the orange épée glowing brightly lighting up the lift tube shaft around her modestly. She cut the inner pocket material out then repeated the procedure on the other pocket fabric. The laser blade went back in the bum bag, then she tugged on the improvised gloves, and climbed the lift tube shaft wall one level.

The ventilation duct above seemed like the only way to exit the lift tube shaft, so Jennifer pushed a toe atop a protruding fitting anchoring a vertical cableway of wires to catch her weight. Using one hand to hold the round conduit, she reached back into the bum bag and flicked on the laser blade again. The soft glow revealed the presence of pressure sensors on the grating. Turning her head to protect her face, she pressed the tip of the L blade to the edge of the grating. This was a trick that Linden had told her might work—a means of disabling the electronic sensors. The quick flash spark proved Linden was right, as did the scorch mark it left behind.

Jennifer removed the grating and clawed her way up into the ventilation system pulling herself along to the first opening. Careful not to do anything that would cause damage to her head, she crawled past the grate then with a solid kick smashed the thin grill out, allowing her to slither into Measures' flat. Her head felt fine, by design. She didn't want to shoulder the vent grate out of its frame, afraid that doing so would cause her skull to rattle with the effort.

Jennifer thought to herself—*I'm trainable, I'm learning: Learning how to take care of my feeble little head.*

Linden had warned her that Measures' flat would have white noise generators and soundproofed walls to shield it. This also meant that Jennifer was truly on her own now. There was no way her HC could communicate through the barriers Measures had erected to protect her illegal business.

Jennifer figured she'd have to disable Measures in order to set up the interrogation. The description of Measures that Linden had provided dictated how that interrogation would be accomplished—carefully! Measures was five-feet-nine, one-hundred-and-seventy pounds of solid muscle. In her previous life she was a bodybuilder. That former lifestyle bled into her current habits meaning that the woman made regular and highly disciplined trips to the gym. Jennifer had NO intention of tussling with a brute like Measures—foolish, very foolish.

Following the floor plan that Linden had provided, she made her way to the walk-in closet in Measures' master suite. The double pocket doors were ajar about four inches. She tugged the left door and pulled it open. At the same time the other door that was connected via the track above uniformly widened the gap allowing her to enter. She pushed the door shut leaving the same slit width.

Closing her eyes, Jennifer pictured what Measures would do once the woman came home from her trip off-world. She would most likely use the WC to relieve herself and maybe freshen up before unpacking. Jennifer listened and waited.

Jennifer's eyes popped open in alarm when sounds came from the master suite beyond. She had not heard even a peep of noise when Measures entered her flat. The soundproofing was very good. Jennifer had already deployed a rather large dose of ketamine, befitting the size of her prey, in the syringe she now held between her fingers. Jennifer took in slow, measured breaths, controlling the adrenaline that had knifed her chest moments earlier.

The angle of view allowed Jennifer to catch a glimpse of the fit woman's broad back as she entered the master WC. Jennifer could barely hear the water run briefly before Measures retreated out of the WC back into the master, her eyes cast in the direction of the bed. Measures moved out of sight apparently unpacking her suitcase. Jennifer was very glad indeed she had decided not to tussle with this woman.

No sooner than Jennifer processed the thought, the pocket door was pulled apart igniting her reflexes. The leading edge of a suitcase was pushed through the opening to be placed on the closet floor. Measures bent down, the side of her rigid neck perched less than two feet from the tip of the syringe. Before the suitcase touched down Jennifer shot her hand out seating the needle home with a hard strike pressing the plunger. The woman pitched forward face first smacking her head into the closet back wall before lashing out instinctively with both arms as if trying to fight off a swarm of bees circling her head. Measures' chest landed on the suitcase with an audible grunt.

Jennifer swiftly retreated, pressing her back against the closet wall, careful to stay out of the path of Measures' powerful forearms swinging wildly but starting to slow. Jennifer focused on what she could control. If her victim was going to inadvertently land a vicious blow Jennifer could not allow that. Her laser blade was out and ready, ready to slice whatever limb happened to be thrust in her direction. There was not a limb to slice. Measures crumpled unconscious atop the suitcase face down.

As Laura Measures' consciousness grew stronger, she realized her arms were bound tightly behind her at both the wrists and elbows. To her strong dismay both nipples were clamped painfully by paper binder clips. The clips were attached to thin wires pulling her chest taught through her T shirt to the legs of the chair she was slumped forward in. Measures felt a hard square wedge under her ass cheeks that was placed atop the chair causing her to lean forward, but only so far. A thin cord of metal wire around her neck was cutting deeply into her skin. Another length of wire was fashioned around her waist pulling her ass back into the chair. Both legs were securely bound to the chair legs with something equally painful. When she started to hyperventilate, the pain of the competing tensions at all these fixed points sent a panic of alarm through her brain.

Holy Shit!

"Awake? Good. I even had enough time to take a nap…" The thin young woman yawned and stretched from a high back office chair in front of her helpless captive.

Jennifer Bane forked another bunch of salad fixin's into her hungry mouth smiling evilly as she munched.

Laura Measures tried to turn her head, searching for a way out, but the effort only snugged the tourniquets pinching her pulsing nipples. When she swallowed, the strained tendons on her throat jumped under the thin razor-like filament around her neck, feeling like a potato peeler shearing off the peel to uncover the soft flesh underneath.

Jennifer swallowed her mouthful, used the napkin in her lap, and eyed Measures casually.

"Effete. I believe that's the word you're searching for, Laura dear."

When no recognition formed behind Measures' panicked eyes Jennifer explained.

"It means sterile," she amended, setting the salad on the credenza behind her.

The laser pistol rested beneath the napkin in Jennifer's lap. She was a good 12 or 14 feet away from Measures in the woman's living room. The distance would give her plenty of time to use it if the need arose.

Jennifer rolled her eyes around the room as if searching it for a weakness.

"Your soundproofing works to my advantage today, Laura. Although I doubt you can find the volume you need to let out a really loud scream with that piano wire around your neck. Wouldn't matter anyway."

Jennifer twisted the corner of her mouth.

"I ripped apart your piano…afraid it's not gonna be in tune until it's repaired. Yes, that really is piano wire clinching your body immobile at several strategic fixed points."

Jennifer stood up but had no intention of taking a step closer to the dangerous woman—at least not yet.

"You have a tendency toward violence that needs to be controlled."

When Measures swallowed the wire pulled blood from her throat. It started to drip slowly.

"I have questions. You sold a floater that hurt someone close to me. As you probably guessed by now, there's only one way to save yourself and live beyond the next day. What'd ya say, Laura? You want to start spilling?"

Jennifer squinted, her voice grime and harsh.

"The fitness that courses through your veins is working against you today. Most women don't have a such a wiry neck like yours." Jennifer lifted her chin and smoothed a hand up and down over her throat. "Mine's got some cushion. Yours is bleeding a bit, I'm afraid. You've got a lot of testosterone in you, don't you?"

Measures tried to speak but her throat had constricted in pain and fear.

"Dream on, Laura," Jennifer blew out. "I'm not gonna loosen the cord around your neck so you can talk easily."

Jennifer turned and grabbed the hand comp on the credenza. She pulled it to her face, then her hateful eyes lifted from the screen pinning Laura Measures into their crosshairs.

"I was able to step out of your flat so that my techy could hack your password. You do most of your work using your HC. I can do that work now."

Measures recognized the HC Jennifer was holding as her own. Her skin started contracting all over her body. Bile crept into her throat, sour as sin.

Jennifer's voice cut into Measures' rising terror as she set the HC back down.

"Once you're dead, I'll be taking your place for a while, and when I'm done, I'll fold up your operation and throw it away. You sell more than just floaters. You market other arms as well."

Measures was helpless to disagree but tried anyway.

"What operation?" She croaked.

When Jennifer tensed she knew she had made a mistake.

"Alright, I did sell a floater off-world. I just don't know who the buyer was. Look! Look on my HC! You'll see the anonymous payment. Go ahead and look. You can confirm what I'm telling you is true. I wouldn't lie to you. No way! No way!"

Measures couldn't stand saying more. The thin cord constricting her throat felt like a cheese grater gnashing her skin with each jerk of cartilage forming a word.

Jennifer sat down and shook her head.

"Laura, this is not going to end well for you," Jennifer stated dangerously. "You had to deliver it to a person. Or was it a *being*? You just returned from off-world. Listen carefully," an apocalyptic warning clearly evident in Jennifer's threatening tone. "Who. Did. You. Sell. It. To!?"

When the answer didn't come, Jennifer reached into her bum bag and pulled out a small black canister about the size of her palm. Holding the laser pistol in one hand and the canister in the other, she made her way in front of Measures.

Jennifer's eyes were searing bolts of heat-stinging gems.

Measures' mouth dropped open but no words came out. Her lower lip quivered.

Jennifer bent down and pointed the LP at one of the petrified woman's eyes, then pointed the canister at the other. The small round ejection port on top of the canister was two inches from Measures' retina.

Jennifer looked into her eyes and shook her head twice.

"This is a trusty stand-by—pepper spray. Old-fashioned but highly effective. The five million Scoville Heat Units won't actually burn your eye out of your skull. It'll just feel like it. The formula is called a legacy formula—maybe old as old Earth itself. Law enforcement probably still carries this stuff on Earth, although I've never been there to verify that."

Jennifer continued quietly, somehow holding back the furor that was causing one corner of her mouth to tick.

"Spill right now, Laura. Don't make me start with this eye then tomorrow work on the other one."

The gulp in Measures' throat sheared a fine filament of skin across the raw nape. The skin accordioned against the taut piano wire pulling blood into each peak and valley of the razor thin flesh bunched against the slender cord.

Measures did not know the answer.

Jennifer realized Measures did not, in fact, know the answer, but as her past had always shown, there was always a cap, a ceiling, a defining limit to her ability to control her poisonous temper. Thinking about Jeffrey lying face down in the mobility bed twitched the flexor tendon in her forearm attached to the trigger finger resting atop the canister.

The pepper spray spit a tight orange stream soaking Measures' open eye.

Jennifer's hate caused the other flexor digitorum superficialis muscle to twitch against the LP trigger stroking off a high pitch *zint* a half-second after the pepper spray deployed. Her arm jerked up just in time to singe Measures' hair. The white bolt of energy grazed her scalp then struck the living room wall with a spark.

A coarse frown split Jennifer's face upset with herself for nearly killing Measures.

Laura Measures howled in pain, clamping her eyes shut against the scorching blaze of stifling heat boiling her eyeball like a poached egg.

Jennifer stood abruptly taking in a harsh breath trying to pull some composure, along with acquittal, back into her chest.

Measures' cries of pain were not penetrating Jennifer's ears. She just looked down at the traumatized woman thinking about how fortunate the bitch was to still be alive.

However I did it, I controlled my actions. I didn't kill her, I didn't, Jennifer acquitted.

Jennifer turned like a robot, still not hearing Measures' screams of agony, carrying a blank look with her out of the living room to the back door to Measures' flat. She pulled the pocket door open and stepped out shuffling a pace sideways, careful to shut the door fast. She leaned back against the door jamb allowing her legs to ease her tense body down to the deck sitting. This was a private little fenced-in area where Measures could sit outside on the roof top of the building. She pulled the vial of meds from her back pocket and dry swallowed two.

Jennifer's HC shuddered in her other back pocket. She reached back and pulled it to her ear.

"Linden," she acknowledged.

"Captain," Linden replied respectfully.

Jennifer blinked at the confirmation of rank. She *was* a privateer captain again. *Was that what pulled the barrel of the laser pistol off target earlier?* Jennifer didn't know, but she did know that she had an obligation to her crew AND to the people that cared about her.

"Captain?" Linden repeated when Jennifer failed to answer.

"I'm here, Linden."

"You alright, Captain?"

People that cared about her…

"Just a little shaky. I pulled a win from what could have otherwise been a screw-up."

"Nice job," he confirmed.

People that counted on her…

"I looked into the abductions more. This will definitely interest you. As you're our only feet dirt-side you may decide to validate what I tell you as true or false…"

Jennifer sat up straighter, her eyes narrowing.

"Measures."

"Yes, Captain. Measures. Your call, but you may want to put her to some good use given she's still alive."

People that knew her well…

"Thanks for not making me explain myself, Linden."

"Listen to this…" Linden continued, filling her in with what he had discovered.

THREE

Laura Measures was out cold. Jennifer had given her a much smaller dose of ketamine after frying her eyeball with the pepper spray. As Jennifer looked down at her on the deck just outside Measures' flat, she did have to say that her right eye looked terrible. The swelling was extensive pulling the eye shut, and would occlude her vision, probably for some days to come.

Jennifer had removed the restraining wires from her captive, slipped on a long-sleeved mock turtle neck to hide her throat, and cleaned her up a bit. The arms dealer could now act as *bait*.

Jennifer intended to test Linden's theory.

No time to waste.

Jennifer stepped over to the corner of the small foyer where the lift tube deposited residents on the seventh floor. Measures' apartment door was one of four resident apartments on the top floor. She reached up as high as her arm would stretch and placed a small remote vid cam on the wall. The barely noticeable vid cam stuck in place in the corner of the foyer giving Jennifer a view of Laura Measures lying just outside her flat.

Jennifer went back inside Measures' residence and pulled herself into the ventilation duck, careful to secure the grate back the way it was before her ingress. She pulled on the makeshift gloves and made her way back to the lift tube shaft. Down the shaft to the top of one of two lift tubes, she pulled up the access hatch, then jumped down into the lift tube and pressed L for Lobby.

Head down, Jennifer walked briskly out of the building lobby across the street and around the back of the building to where her rental air car was parked. Safely inside, Jennifer fired up the vid cam receiver on her own HC and the small screen crackled to life showing the foyer on the seventh floor where she had left Measures unconscious. She set her HC aside on the passenger seat.

Jennifer pulled out Measures' hand comp, fingered the screen, and waited until she heard the comm she had just placed connect.

"Emergency services!" Jennifer feigned panic in her voice. "I live at Brash Tower, on Abalong Street. I'm just leaving my flat and found my neighbor lying in the foyer on the seventh floor. She's injured! Send help quick!"

Jennifer cut the feed before the dispatcher could start asking questions. While she waited for the medicos to respond, Measures' HC warbled unexpectedly. The comm ID said GUNNY.

Jennifer spoke into the HC activating the voice app to accept the message.

"Yeah, what's up?" Jennifer spoke into the HC responding to GUNNY, whoever GUNNY was. The HC voice app typed a reply sending it off.

"When'd you get back dirt-side?" GUNNY's message displayed on screen.

Thinking quickly, Jennifer responded verbally into the HC to send another message.

"A few hours ago. I've got another lead, another customer. I need some more hardware." Jennifer bared open her desire to purchase more arms from GUNNY, intuitively matching the moniker with the person's business. Jennifer crossed her fingers and waited to see if she was right.

The person on the other end hesitated twenty seconds or so then asked, "Alright, what do you need?"

Jennifer sent GUNNY a list that she had previously found on Measures' hand comp when she inspected it prior to interrogating her. The list of munitions was lengthy and deadly but not overly so. Twelve total pieces on the order.

GUNNY didn't seem to have a problem with the order.

"This'll cost you. Just like before," was the short message response.

"I need it today," Jennifer replied.

There was at least a full minute delay, then,"No can do. Too quick."

"Okay. I have other sources." Jennifer turned the screw a bit to see if it hurt.

"Oh, please. I know you. You never need equipment this fast. Just wait a few days like always."

Jennifer responded quickly, simply.

"No."

The first real bit of information came back from GUNNY.

"Is this for the same client as the floater?"

"I don't even know who got that floater." Jennifer repeated what Laura Measures didn't know.

"What do you mean?"

"I just don't know! I've developed my own client relationship and I want to satisfy this new client. Simple as that. You gonna help me or not?" Maybe a little push would help. If Jennifer could convince this person to meet perhaps she could get more info on who was buying munitions and why.

"You always were a bitch, Laura."

Jennifer assumed that about Measures from second one. *Glad I'm not alone.*

"I'm waiting…" Jennifer prodded, hoping GUNNY would bite.

A full two minutes passed, then,"Meet me at the same place. It'll be late, though. 2am."

"No." *Since Measures was a bitch, why stop now?* Besides, there was a reason Jennifer declined.

"No? What do you mean, no?"

"I mean NO, not at the same place. Yes, to the 2am." Jennifer did not know the location of the meet to pick up the hardware. That is why she declined. Despite scouring Measures' HC there was no address for any sort of munitions pick up location.

"Why?" Suspicious, sure.

"I'm a bitch, remember?" Jennifer let GUNNY stew on that for a minute.

Then the reply came back.

"Okay, back up location then."

Shit! Jennifer cursed to herself. *I don't know that place either.*

"Forget it. I'm waisting time here. This one I'll get from another supplier." Jennifer didn't know what to do. This was all she could think of.

Very quickly GUNNY replied.

"Wait!"

Jennifer smiled, *Greedy aren't we?*

Jennifer shot a message to tighten the screw a half-turn more. *No point backing down now.*

"I'm waiting."

"Waiting for what, Laura? You expect me to expose myself, my operation just because you're on your period today? FU!"

"I will not trade sexual favors for equipment. You know me better than that." Jennifer tried to lighten the mood a bit—maybe that would loosen GUNNY's screw.

"We're talking in circles here, Laura. What the hell do you want from me? I won't put my business at risk 'cause you're PMSing!"

Still not working. Okay, time to threaten something that may not even be a threat.

"I can't lose this client. If I do, you lose me as one. End of story."

"You damn bitch!"

"Yep."

Thirty seconds passed.

"What exactly do you want, Laura? Besides the equipment?"

"I want to meet at a place of my choosing this time. Terms have changed."

No sense in NOT pushing this transaction to the limit. I only have something to gain here, was all Jennifer could think. *Besides, the first responders are gonna be here any minute and following THEM is the real play this afternoon.*

After a minute the reply came. "Where then?"

"I'll let you know later, just get the stuff ready." Jennifer cut the comm leaving GUNNY to chew on that slap in the face. All things being equal, she had made progress and not shown weakness. Just looking at Laura Measures told her that weakness was not a part of her persona. Jennifer would figure out a way to meet GUNNY and get what information she could.

Meanwhile…

The air ambulance would be arriving any minute. Jennifer fired up the air car grav gen and pulled out of the back alley turning left twice to put her on Abalong Street. She cut the grav gen, parking down the street from the entrance to Brash Tower. The air ambulance was already there.

Jennifer pulled her HC from the passenger seat studying the screen. Two EMTs were lifting Measures onto an anti grav gurney. What was odd about the scene was that the procedure did not look practiced, or fluid—far from it.

One medico grabbed Measures' ankles roughly, one in each hand, then the other EMT looped his arms through her arm pits. They lifted in staggered succession, not seeming to coordinate their maneuver in unison. Measures' butt, back and head landed clumsily on the gurney, then the EMT at her feet simply let go of her ankles plopping her legs down next. If the patient wasn't already injured, it looked like they sure would be now. The two EMTs didn't even slap a blood pressure cuff on Measures or check O_2 level or heart rate—nothing.

Linden had warned Jennifer about something like this. Well, not something about how clumsy the first responders were, only that Jennifer should look for signs for how inexperienced they might be. Her Chief Security Officer seemed to have nailed that one. *Wow! He's still really good at his job,* Jennifer appraised to herself.

One of the responders fired up the anti grav gurney and guided it into the open lift tube. About a minute-and-a-half later Jennifer pulled her eyes from her HC screen to see the two EMTs exit the lobby following the gurney to the rear of the air ambulance. The double doors opened and the gurney floated in, followed by the EMTs.

Jennifer knew for a fact that on another planet emergency service vehicles were allowed to travel above roof top level. On the planet Basley, which was the home planet of her husband Krachy, there were at least four slots that traffic could use. The higher the air vehicle went, the less traffic there was. Civilian traffic used slot one, air cars with two or more could use the high occupancy slot two, delivery vehicles in slot three, and emergency vehicles slot four. Emergency vehicles on Basley could interpret slot four as *anywhere* in the sky.

Jennifer didn't know the rules for this planet, however. It was her very first visit dirt-side here. Although by the looks of a few air cars passing by above on Abalong, Beltina had at least a slot two.

If the air ambulance used slot four and darted up above building level, Jennifer had a real chance of losing them. She didn't have any type of homing beacon that she could affix to the air ambulance to track its location, so if it went too high, and too fast, this was going to be a very short surveillance tail.

Jennifer started up her air car and pulled out when slot one was clear following the air ambulance as it made a quick right turn close to the ground. After a few more turns it seemed that the vehicle was not going to shoot up into the city sky and blaze off toward a hospital. The air ambulance stayed in slot one.

Linden had told Jennifer to expect this. To expect the air ambulance NOT to head straight to a hospital. But Linden did not cover what altitude the *imitation* EMTs would use to get to their destination. It was already becoming clear that these first responders were not the real deal.

These fake EMTs were very inexperienced indeed. So much so that they stayed in slot one all the way to the outskirts of the city and into the sparsely populated suburbs. They weren't headed to a hospital, no way.

Jennifer followed along at a safe distance her heart beating faster. These people, these imposters, were very sure of themselves. That was clear. What they had just done, the way they traveled in the air ambulance, only helped confirm Linden's suspicions that these people were not EMTs at all.

Since these connivers didn't bother to travel at a high altitude, it meant that they weren't even worried about being noticed for what they DID NOT do—travel above building level.

All of the above gave Jennifer much more pause than when her security officer first revealed his theory. Linden had to be right. Since he was right, there was a real danger that anyone that took notice of these abnormalities, this lack of following even the most simple of emergency procedures, would be considered a threat. Jennifer did not have the extra firepower she had ordered from GUNNY, nor did she have any backup dirt-side. Alarm bells clambered in her head.

Jennifer eased off the throttle as the scenery on the outskirts of Sommerville gave way to more countryside. She did not want to expose herself any more than necessary.

Thankfully there was sparse traffic. Since the air ambulance didn't have on its strobe lights, other traffic didn't pull aside letting it past. This made it much easier to follow.

This simple fact made Jennifer even more nervous.

The people Jennifer had just witnessed commit an abduction seemed confident that no one would deter them.

FOUR

Jennifer's hand comp vibrated and she plucked it from the passenger seat.

"What's your status, Captain?" Linden Kay asked.

"I've got a tail going on the air ambulance, but I'm holding back, as per your instructions. I don't want to expose myself to find out their destination. From what you said this is only one of many such fake first responder abduction teams. This is putting the creep willies in me big time, Linden. I don't like what all this shit implies."

"Good," Linden replied. "You're right. Do not get spotted. This operation is large. It's not worth risking your life to find their location until you're certain you can do it covertly."

Jennifer opened her mouth to disagree, her force of personality starting to override good sense, but Linden's tone turned hard.

"Back off, back off! Abort, Captain!"

"I'm out in the countryside and exposed," Jennifer responded, convincing herself with the statement that Linden was right. Then, "Copy that, I'm bailing out—"

Up ahead the air ambulance made a hard break check forcing the air car following it to swerve. The ambulance banked hard in a U-turn, already pointed down the other lane, picking up speed coming back in her direction.

Jennifer was taken aback for a moment, but then she pulled her laser pistol from the bum bag gripping the handle and stroking her finger on the trigger ready to act.

The air ambulance barreled past, paying her no attention whatsoever, heading back toward the city fast.

Jennifer released her clinched sphincter and breathed out.

"He's heading back toward the city. Picking up speed. My cover is still good."

"They're going back for another pickup—another abduction."

What? How does my cyber expert know that?

Before Jennifer could ask, Linden explained.

"Low hanging fruit, Captain. They got another dispatch and are headed to that location fast to make their trip today a twofer—two for the price of one. Measures and some other poor bastard."

Jennifer pushed aside her confusion about how Linden's cyber wizardry deduced this play. All she knew was that she trusted him implicitly.

"Copy that." She had already swung her air car around in pursuit.

Back in the city limits the air ambulance made steady progress through the winding streets to a very run down and grimy part of Sommerville, basically a ghetto. The vehicle started to slow as Jennifer spotted a young woman slumped against an abandoned store front on the other side of the street.

There was no one else around, the street deserted.

The air ambulance didn't stop across the street from the woman, instead choosing to head to the next stop crossing to make a U-turn and come back for the pickup.

The air ambulance was going to abduct the woman slumped against the building! It had to be.

Jennifer darted her air car left into the stop crossing just up the street from the woman. Her maneuver pushed her vehicle past the corner of the abandoned building shielding it from being seen by the air ambulance coming towards the woman.

In a fluid and instinctual set of movements Jennifer acted.

She punched the boot release button on her way out of the opening driver side door.

LP still in hand, she shoved it into her waistband, already reaching for the flechette rifle in the boot.

Jennifer shouldered the weapon, and in six long fast strides sighted the driver of the air ambulance from the corner of the building.

She cross-haired the driver, resting the rifle against the building corner, and milked the trigger twice. Darts penetrated the windshield and tore into the chest of the driver, the man's dying reflex yanking the control stick hard, forcing the van up over the curb. With no wheels, the van's careening journey smashed it into the building front not eight feet from the collapsed woman.

Jennifer swept her rifle to a second man coming around one of the open back doors and punched a single 7mm dart through his ear. The fake responder tumbled face-first to the ceramacrete eliciting a cry of dismay.

The last man exploded around the back of the van, crouching low in response to Jennifer's marksmanship.

Jennifer dropped and rolled on her shoulders as an energy bolt belched violently in her direction. The corner of the brick building splintered pellet shards.

Jennifer completed her shoulder roll and came up in a half-crouch, the laser pistol now in hand, popping out a high pitched *zint* into the face of the gunner.

The dead man tumbled across a garbage can deforming the container's thin metal skin. His LP clattered to the sidewalk.

Jennifer ran over to the man she'd clipped through the ear and lashed out with the butt of her LP, the solid pistol's grip cracking across the man's jaw as he looked up.

Stunned, the shooter was helpless as Jennifer plucked the weapon he'd used from the ground beside him. He was bleeding from the ear and pistol whip. His eyes took in the dangerous look on Jennifer's face and foolishly considered another attack.

"Don't!" Jennifer ordered.

Jennifer clubbed the man again, this shot aimed at the injured man's temple. The man slumped to the pavement like a sack of laundry.

The young woman peered at the scene in front of her, her face a mask of terror as she observed the carnage Jennifer had wrought.

"Get up and get into my air car," Jennifer instructed.

The woman pulled herself standing shakily then steadied an outstretched hand on the building before half-stumbling around the corner of the building toward the air car. Jennifer met the woman halfway and helped the disoriented woman into the passenger seat.

Safely inside, Jennifer turned fast running around the building corner and was back in no time dragging the unconscious guy she'd shot by the legs. She grunted and heaved the awkward body into the boot. Jennifer disappeared again then returned guiding the anti grav gurney with Laura Measures on it around the building to the back of her air car. She fingered the small control panel on the cross bar of the gurney, pitching the unconscious woman forward into the boot atop the man like a loader bucket on a tractor expelling its load. She closed the boot, picked up the rifle, then jumped behind the controls powering the air car quickly down the street.

Jennifer looked over at the young woman, said softly, almost soothingly, "They were coming for you but you're safe now."

She looked up at the taller woman, brown eyes wide and fearful.

Jennifer realized the woman was most likely high on drugs, on something, and still not processing the whole episode.

"I knew they were coming for you. I don't want to hurt you at all," she soothed. "You understand?"

The woman looked at the hand Jennifer had briefly placed on her shoulder, then back into her eyes.

"I understand." Then she glanced out the front windshield. "I know where to go, take a right."

"I figured as much," Jennifer answered. "You being in this part of town alone means you know the area. Right?"

The woman flicked a look at her before returning her gaze out the windshield.

"Yes."

Jennifer nodded and followed the woman's directions to an underpass over a wide water runoff spillway. She powered down the air car under the dark and desolate bridge, then looked over at the woman. She was fast asleep having nodded off after providing the last bit of guidance to their destination.

Jennifer startled herself awake with a jerk. The post-combat adrenaline dump had hit her hard. The last thing she remembered was swallowing two pills after watching the sleeping woman beside her in the air car. It was dark now. The 28-hour Beltina day meant that nighttime was long—a good 13 hours or more.

Jennifer swiveled her head surveying the underpass she was parked beneath. To her right was the sloping ceramacrete arch of the bridge support, and to her left, across the trickling rivulet of slimy water in the spillway, people were gathered. They were huddled around what looked like a fire underneath a large foil roasting tray with food in it. The arch on the other side had a mural on it. *Strange*, Jennifer thought to herself. *I don't remember seeing that mural before I fell asleep.*

Jennifer yawned hard then rubbed her neck. It was sore from the awkward position of her hasty nap, or from the shoulder roll during the shootout, she couldn't tell. The pills must have knocked her out pulling the adrenaline from her taught muscles as a result of the firefight. Her head seemed okay, so no big problem.

Just then she noticed she was alone in the air car. On second thought, *I am not okay. I didn't even notice the woman was gone when I woke up.* However, this was nothing new for Jennifer. Her head trauma was a new normal in her life. She often misplaced events in sequence. The cumulative nature of her injuries was deteriorating her ability to slot time accurately. These chronic symptoms manifested themselves as early stages of Alzheimer's Disease.

Jennifer got out the air car and walked slowly toward the people. She hesitated for a full minute at the foot-wide stream of water, not sure how to navigate the simple obstacle, with her head pounding between her ears. An arm looped through her elbow.

Jennifer turned looking down into the concerned eyes of the woman she had rescued.

"Here, let me help you." The short woman tugged gently at Jennifer's arm stepping over the water flow with ease. Jennifer followed suit, using her much longer stride, after seeing it demonstrated.

The flickering light of the fire made for an eerie projection of light up the face of the curving under-arch of the bridge. Jennifer stopped short of the people, now pushing spoonfuls of food into their mouths, and looked up trying to focus on the mural.

Confusion constricted Jennifer's chest pausing her next inhale. The mural was a caricature of a powerful muscle-bound woman gripping a rifle across her chest fearlessly. The exaggerated muscles bulged from under a crew-neck black long sleeved top. The mighty portrayal of muscular legs pushed the limits of the blue trousers. Jennifer pulled in a breath…squinting at the face of the woman. The dim firelight pierced the darkness revealing the sharp details of the heroine's face…It was her!

Jennifer started to shiver even though the night was warm.

The homeless people stopped eating and moved away from the campfire meal quickly.

The woman held Jennifer's arm tighter and asked a simple question.

"What's your name?"

The calm in the woman's question pulled some reality back into this very surreal setting.

Jennifer concentrated on speaking clearly, cleared her throat.

"Jennifer."

"I'm Darla. Nice to meet you." Darla smiled genuinely. "Would you like to sit down, Jennifer?" She tugged her elbow toward one of the tattered chairs next to the fire.

Jennifer blinked staring at the woman.

"Yes."

The two of them sat down. Jennifer helped herself grabbing some of what looked like stir-fry veggies and rice from the foil tray. She didn't use a spoon, just dipping her cupped palm into the cuisine, then shoveling warm food into her ravenous mouth. Jennifer started to calm down as she ate more.

"I don't deserve, I mean I'm nobody importan—"

Darla looked up at the flickering light illuminating the mural then over at Jennifer. She was about five-two, with very dark skin and a gently sloping forehead. Her young cheeks were smooth and her jaw wide, revealing large teeth in a friendly smile. Her hair was short, dark, course, and tightly coiled, bordering on ropey, due to its thickness. She was maybe 18 or 19 years old.

Darla's dark brown eyes gathered Jennifer in.

"Of course you're important. All of us here are. Go ahead and eat some more. I'll get us some water."

Jennifer couldn't stop eating. Maybe it was to keep herself occupied trying not to think about what these people thought of her, or maybe it was because she was scared to death that she was getting sicker every day. And that she had no control of her decline—none. Whatever the reason, she stuffed herself, and swigged at the water bottle while her and Darla talked.

Darla had a soothing, somewhat spiritual way about her.

"How did you know they'd come for me?"

"I was tailing them after I let them kidnap the woman they were transporting." Just then it hit Jennifer that one of the EMT thugs and Laura Measures were still in the boot.

Jennifer bristled.

"There are two people in the boot!" Her eyes looked pan-icked, as though the captives were free, and about to form up for an attack.

Darla smiled.

"Don't worry, they're under guard. They won't hurt us."

Jennifer pursed her lips and looked down.

"I totally forgot they were in the boot until just now, Darla," she admitted, head still down. Her face lifted. "I get real sick sometimes."

"I do too. I was real sick when you showed up and stopped them. You risked a lot to save me. Thank you."

"Darla, I shouldn't stay here. I'm just putting you, put-ting all of you at risk." Jennifer jerked her head side-to-side. "I should go. I bring trouble with me everywhere I go. I came dirt-side alone NOT to do that. To put others at risk."

"You're off to a good start then."

"What?"

"I'm not at risk. I was, but you stopped them. I want to offer you something."

When Jennifer sat up straighter, refusing any type of gift in her posture, Darla continued quickly.

"I want to offer you a base of operation, Jennifer. Not a gift. Nothing like that."

"The meal was plenty, thank you. I'm gonna go." When Jennifer stood the nausea in her head caused her to swallow several times. She sat back down.

"You should rest some more," Darla concluded. "I'll help you over to your air car. You can recline the seat this time and pass out. No one will bother you. Let's go."

Darla stood and walked with Jennifer back over to the air car.

Jennifer had no strength to argue. She was exhausted. She climbed into the passenger side of the rental, and almost before her torso reclined in the seat, her eyes snapped shut.

When Jennifer woke it was morning. The sun was low and had not risen above the sides of the spillway.

She had to pee bad, so she got out and made her way out from under the bridge relieving herself pretty much out in the open.

Just to convince herself of something that was still bugging her, Jennifer went to the back of the air car and opened the lid on the boot. She was shocked to see the trunk filled with armaments.

What the hell?

A voice behind Jennifer said.

"You left Measures' HC unlocked after you used it."

Jennifer wheeled around to find Darla standing behind her with a dirty blanket wrapped around her body.

"I picked up the stuff from GUNNY."

Jennifer was not sick now, just utterly confused. She parked her rump on the trunk frame staring at the shorter woman in disbelief.

"Just because I don't have a home, doesn't mean I'm stupid, Jennifer." She smirked.

"Obviously."

"You want to know WHERE I met him. Ha," Darla laughed. "Getting a good location out of Measures was easy. I threatened to cook her other eye. She told me the back up meet location willingly. I had GUNNY drop the booty and leave so I could slide in and pick it up unseen…" She smiled showing her white teeth. "Then I had a few friends follow him. I guess he's not used to Measures having backup," Darla cocked her head. "His mistake."

Jennifer's eyes could not have held more fascination.

Darla continued.

"I spoke with him, in person."

"You did?"

"You didn't read into or interpret the conversation you had with him on Measures' HC very well," Darla commented.

When Jennifer's look glazed over, Darla summed it up succinctly.

"Greed, Jennifer, greed. I commed him, acting as Measures, and told him the order had a mistake. He disagreed so I threatened to leave all the stuff where I picked it up, pull the payment, AND share his home address with several Newsy outlets." She half shrugged. "He was back in 30 minutes. I was alone, and didn't pose a threat, so he approached me and I told him that Measures wouldn't be buying from him any longer. I told him there was a new player in the game. And if he wanted to forge a relationship and protect his business he'd better bargain with me."

"He bit?" She asked hesitantly, unable to control her curiosity.

Darla explained what she worked out with GUNNY. Jennifer listened intently, clearly intrigued. The ploy GUNNY agreed to be a part of just might work.

When Darla was done, Jennifer's face still held concern. She wasn't convinced and didn't want to put Darla or her friends at risk. Although after Darla's outing, that was going to be pretty damn hard to avoid now.

"You were the one that provided access to Measures' bank account," Darla mentioned. "I paid him double the order after our meet. He knew I had backup. How else could I have gotten his address? There was no way he was going to test me. He likes being in business. Besides," Darla pulled down her brows, the corners of her mouth rising, "He thinks Measures is a real bitch."

Darla glanced down into the boot then back up at Jennifer.

"NOW you think you have what you need to continue this thing?"

FIVE

"It's not what you have done, it's what needs to be done, Jennifer," Darla said.

Jennifer pulled herself off the air car trunk frame standing straight.

"I didn't know that those men were coming for you specifically. I would have done what I did for anyone in that situation. And it goes deeper than that. I had someone I care about nearly killed because of Laura Measures. She sold a floater that was meant to get me but instead injured my sworn vassal who shielded me from the blast."

Jennifer's look turned distant.

"What I did yesterday was because of his example. You're giving me way too much credit. I don't exactly know what needs to be done. You seem to have a better idea about that than me."

Jennifer's head turned surveying the armaments in the boot for a moment before looking back at Darla.

"Just because I have access to all this, doesn't mean I can make the kind of difference you seem to think I can. These are just tools. The scheme you got GUNNY to agree to could expose you and your friends. You understand?"

Darla walked over to the boot resting a hand on the tailgate looking at the weapons. She removed her hand and directed a rather ominous glare at Jennifer.

"Act locally, think globally."

Jennifer's forehead grooved.

"You're saying I'm thinking too big?"

Darla nodded silently.

"I want to work on what we have control over. You should do that too."

"You know, I've had this kind of advice before. From many sides." Jennifer's cheek twisted ironically. "I've started out on things like this before. Yesterday I convinced myself that I'm learning, that I'm trainable. You seemed to have figured me out easily. I must be shallow."

One of Darla's cheeks inched up.

"Not shallow…driven."

"I've already told you that I'll bring more trouble for you, for all of you. There's no question of it! What you don't know is that your prime minister knows me, knows my history. He wants my help."

"With what?"

"There is a new race of beings called Insect Aliens. Lad Blanconales wants to integrate the IAs into Beltina. Have them be a part of your planet. I've not spoken with him, so I don't know why. What I do know is that these creatures are capable of telepathy. They can read minds, Darla. This a powerful trait. I've seen what it's capable of doing—both good and bad. I also know that these creatures have splinter factions with their own agenda. Their entire race does not think alike as was originally discovered. You put all these things together and I shuddered when I was told that Blanconales wanted me to be the go between.

"Doing that, acting like a race broker, is not something I can physically do. As soon as my vassal asked me to consider taking on that job, someone tried to kill me with that floater Laura Measures sold.

"I've run away from dealing with the bad things these Insect Aliens have done in the past. And I'm not looking forward to risking more lives trying to find out why your planet AND them all of a sudden want to join forces."

"How did you first get in the middle of this?"

"I was one of the first people that discovered them. I'm a privateer captain with my own crew and my own ship. Years ago when your planet was at war with Markem, I helped broker a truce to stop the war. I had no choice at the time. I can't tell you how fortunate I was that it worked out the way it did. During all that, I discovered the Insect Alien race. I even have an ongoing relationship with two of the IAs. They act as bodyguards from time-to-time. They helped Jeffrey protect me yesterday."

Jennifer pinched her lips together.

"So here I am today, back in the middle of something that I decided to take on alone so that no one else around me gets hurt. Behind me are enough weapons to start up a nice little war. I'm not saying I don't appreciate what you did, what you've set up with GUNNY, I'm saying that you and your friends may not live to see how this whole thing turns out. People that have worked with me in the past have been injured, Darla. I just told you what happened to my vassal."

"And two fake EMTs died yesterday working against you," Darla bared her teeth.

"I did a good job extracting you and I'm proud of that. Maybe you should consider letting me have that win. That way I can carry on with my selfish little vendetta avenging Jeffrey."

"Jennifer," Darla shook her head, "What we're going to get into together is not going to play out the way you think."

Jennifer was angered by this young woman's certainty. It reminded her of Carol's holier-than-thou attitude.

What have I done to meet another big sister type that thinks she knows what's best? This woman is barely past puberty!

"You have quite a low opinion of my abilities, don't you?" Jennifer's eyes rounded.

"No I don't. Far from it actually."

"I'm sorry I said it like that. It's not all my fault it came out that way. I have a background too. When you live like I do you have to be quick, you have to read people fast, or you may not get a chance to do it again. When you found me yesterday I was having a serious drug withdrawal. The episodes are getting fewer and farther between but they still happen. I was out cold until I heard that van wreck."

"I'm glad you're fighting to get better. Can't you and I just focus on that, focus on you being able to continue that fight, instead of teaming up against who knows what?"

"I can tell that you don't know what's been happening on-planet for the last two months."

"So I guess you're going to tell me to guilt me into going through with this then, righ—?"

As soon as Jennifer said it she regretted it. Her hand went to her mouth covering it from sticking another foot inside.

"Don't do that. You have a temper, Jennifer. I get it."

Jennifer's eyes remained skeptical. She removed her hand.

"There's been a complete and total breakdown in public trust. This was inevitable given people are scared to death to call emergency services, to call first responders, of any type."

"It's that bad?"

"This is much bigger than what you stopped yesterday. It's planet wide. There's near total panic in all the cities on Beltina. The abductions using first responders posing as medical personnel are new. The initial wave of abductions started with security services—policing. Fake security teams started taking people and sometimes families.

"Planet-wide mistrust caused people to arm themselves. Now *real* first responders are getting killed because when they show up to a call for service, people don't know if the responder is real or not."

"Why hasn't Blanconales declared martial law then?"

"That's just it. Who can people trust? Will the security teams deployed be real or fake? Would the public be able to trust the deployed security teams to restore order or would these teams fool people and commit more abductions?"

"Why are people being abducted?"

"I didn't have a theory until just now."

Jennifer squinted shielding her eyes from the rays of sun inching over the spillway wall.

"What then, Darla?"

"The integration of the IAs you mentioned, Jennifer."

Jennifer shifted her weight from foot to foot.

"Could be. So why don't we just ask the fake EMT we captured yesterday?"

"I already asked him about who's behind this. He didn't say a thing about aliens—nothing. He's a peon, not much to tell."

"…And?"

"He was heading to a location to drop off Laura Measures before he turned around to come and abduct me. I didn't get an address."

Jennifer clinched her fists.

"Maybe you didn't ask hard enough."

The corners of Darla's mouth turned down.

"I think you should choose the right way to approach that."

Jennifer's nostrils flared. She dipped her head once.

"That's what needs to be done." She agreed.

***

After cleaning up, eating, and changing clothes, Jennifer had renewed energy. The impressive selection of armaments Darla provided gave her options. She spent the rest of the morning deploying items that would aid in her next foray.

Now she clung to the shadows in the convoluted alleys in Darla's ghetto. She wanted to test a theory of her own. Jennifer's movements through the gnarled maze were steady. She knew where she was going. She had been to the location the day before. Her destination was the wrecked air ambulance from the day before.

Staying concealed at the end of the block, Jennifer spotted the wreck. Her point of view didn't give her a view of the far side of the damaged vehicle, so she couldn't tell if the dead body was still lying on the pavement beyond. No matter.

Jennifer was about to make her move when she spotted movement.

Several homeless people were up the block across the street from the wrecked air ambulance. She waited until they were well clear.

Jennifer emerged from the shadows and ran the half block to the back door of the dormant van, activated an incendiary boomer, then tossed it in the back.

She was almost back to her hide when the metal buckling concussion echoed violently off the surrounding buildings. Back down the alley, staying tight to the shadows, Jennifer turned one, then several more corners before seeing her air car.

Behind the controls she powered up the grav gen advancing the air car directly away from the fire she had just created. A fire she created on purpose, on purpose to elicit a very specific emergency services response.

She finally pulled over and snagged her hand comp from the console pecking in a few commands to pull up the overhead floater drone camera. Jennifer had deployed the floater earlier to survey the air ambulance wreck site. The view was over eight-hundred feet above the burning vehicle. The smoke obscured her ability to again check to see if the dead body was still close by.

She waited.

Sure enough a fire department responder came rushing down the street in an air firetruck.

Jennifer's theory was simple to test: Were firefighters a part of this conspiracy too? Were firefighters abducting people as well?

Jennifer thumbed her hand comp activating the auto hover on the floater drone cam. With the exception of some intermittent wind, the image remained centered on the screen.

Laura Measures' HC was already powered up along with the app that controlled the remote weapon station online that Jennifer had also deployed that morning. The remote tripod mounted weapon was chambered with explosive tipped 12 mm darts. Jennifer had placed the weapon across the street and down the block from the air ambulance wreck, aiming it through an open window on the second floor of an abandoned building. She now looked through the target camera reticle and sighted the air firetruck.

After the dangers of the firefight she engaged in the day before, she had decided to remain in the relative protection of her air car while using the remote weapon.

The firefighters passed the wreck spotting the four homeless people Jennifer had seen a few minutes earlier. If Jennifer's guess was right, the faux firefighters would ignore the air ambulance fire and target the people for abduction instead.

The remote weapon had an auto track feature that kept the air firetruck in the crosshairs. The firefighters did not stop to put out the fire. Apparently they had not been informed that the wrecked air ambulance had been taken out and the crew killed the day before. That was the last mistake the fake firefighting crew would ever make.

The air firetruck was making a straight line for the homeless people to commit an abduction when Jennifer opened fire. The well-aimed sustained auto fire of the flechette machine gun devastated the drive cab on the front of the air truck. One woman that had been holding onto a grab bar at the back of the vehicle jumped to the ground in a tuck and roll. When she came up limping, Jennifer tracked the lethal crosshairs in her direction. The first burst of darts turned the woman's stomach into a blast crater as at least two exploding darts smashed deeply through her intestines. Jennifer saw blood vomit from her lips as she tumbled back slamming to the pavement.

Movement in the sight caught Jennifer's attention, and she stroked the screen rattling off at least two dozen more darts, cracking through what had to be the last of the four-person crew. The devastating force of the mini bombs reduced the fleeing fake firefighter to a cloud of misty blood and pulverized tissue floating in the air from the savage onslaught.

Jennifer tracked the crosshairs to the air firetruck driver cab. It was unrecognizable. No life evident.

Before recalling the overhead floater drone, she panned and zoomed trying to spot the homeless people she'd seen earlier. Due to the sudden and brutal attack on the fake responders, the four homeless people were scrambling in a panic, legs moving fast carrying them out of the area.

Satisfied the people were safe now and were not going to be abducted, Jennifer recalled the floater drone. She did not, however, power down the remote weapon system. She had another use for it. About a minute later Jennifer looked up spotting the arrow-head shaped drone clear the top of the building she was temporarily parked behind. The floater was about 15 inches down each side with a built in anti grav harness for propulsion. She guided it down past the already open boot lid, into the boot, cut the grav gen, then slammed the lid shut before hopping back behind the controls.

Jennifer made a fast right in the air car navigating the serpentine narrow back alleys of *D ghetto*, as Jennifer called it in her head now, to the back of the building where the remote weapon was stationed. She jumped out of the air car, ran over to the tattered back door to the building, bounded through fast, then climbed the set of rickety stairs two at a time. Jennifer turned the corner and spotted the remote weapon sitting harmlessly on its tripod inert. She pulled out the hand comp controlling the deadly rifle and pressed at the toggle controlling the barrel tip. The small servo controlling the rotation of the weapon whined robotically turning the sight of the barrel to the left 80 degrees. The sound of the servo whine cut off abruptly. The silence in the room was ominous given the violence that had erupted from the device only minutes earlier.

There were four round metal support beams uniformly spaced in the rectangular room. Bound tightly against the beam five feet in front of the barrel tip of the machine rifle was the fake EMT that Jennifer had captured the day before. His neck was pinched under two looping ropes of simple power cords cinching his neck against the upright support. Both arms were similarly cuffed with more loops of the wire around his forehead, waist, and ankles, stapling these body parts to the rusty metal support. His bug-eyes were wild with terror but they were not focused on Jennifer—they were locked onto the barrel tip of the machine rifle pointed directly at his stomach.

"One question," Jennifer touched the screen of the HC, jiggling the barrel of the rifle a twitch left then right before centering the sight back to the man's gut.

The nearly hysterical man darted his moist panicked eye-balls at Jennifer, the barrel tip, and back.

Jennifer's voice was as calm as a country pond at daybreak.

"Address of the drop off location for abducted people."

The man tried to respond, his words hypertonic and breathy—not audible from a distance.

Jennifer took three fast strides at her captive dipping her left ear in front of his mouth.

"Say again," she ordered.

She listened carefully squinting her eyes in deep concentration.

Jennifer was not a sadist. But her outrage about the group that this man belonged to was forcing her to act as though she was. She accepted that. And early that same morning Jennifer had also accepted her responsibility.

The crossroad Jennifer had arrived at was self-inflicted. There were two directions now: strength or weakness. It was clear that weakness would put more people at risk.

Jennifer backed up a few paces, pulled the HC to her face, and placed a finger over the fire button.

Her eyes never left the safety of the hand comp screen, and her ears subconsciously clogged the hysterical man's pleading whimpers from registering in her brain.

Almost.

A full minute passed.

Jennifer was unable to press fire to end his life.

Blinders affixed preventing a sideways glance at her upright captive, Jennifer swiftly stepped over to the tripod, folded it up, and retreated back out the way she'd come with the weapon.

The equipment safely stowed in the boot, Jennifer considered what to do with the detainee's life she had just saved. Her outstretched hands held her leaning weight on the boot lid, head down.

She looked up, spotted the door leading back into the building, and came to a decision.

The petrified man was conscious, but could not turn his head. Only his bloodshot eyes tracked her as she came into view. Jennifer halted in front of him.

The two people were the same height.

Sweat streamed down the man's face. His bulging eyes shot a darting glance at the laser blade in Jennifer's hand. His bladder released soaking his pants.

Jennifer's glower precipitated all these events. Her eyes held more than fire; they held a holocaust of warning.

She snapped on the laser blade, then sliced the two ribbons around the man's constricted neck.

The man gasped, and choked, finally able to pull air through his sore windpipe.

With his forehead still secured firmly to the post, he had nowhere to look but straight into Jennifer's viperous eyes.

The scathing resonance of her words seemed to originate from the netherworld.

"There's nowhere you can hide. Nowhere I won't find you. Stop what you've been doing. Do right from now on or be dead. Simple choice," Jennifer pronounced.

She took a step closer.

"Have you made your choice?"

"Yes," the man answered, trembling. "I want to live."

The man took a moment to realize that death had passed on him today. He had every intention of keeping his word.

Jennifer cut the rest of the cords binding the man setting him free, turned and left.

Back in the air car Jennifer got moving.

This attack would bring attention. Two attacks at the same place one day apart. Word and warning would now spread that there was NO low hanging fruit in D ghetto. Consequently, Darla's simple suggestion to act locally and think globally now held special meaning for the group doing the abductions.

By design, definitely by design, Jennifer thought grimly.

SIX

Jennifer sat in the air car waiting and watching. She was in the corner of the parking lot of a restaurant/repair shop twelve miles from the address of the holding site the fake EMT had given her that morning. The eating place had a one-garage air car repair station attached to one side. It looked like a guy worked as a mechanic; he was under an air car up on an anti grav lift applying his trade at the moment. It was 1pm, and Jennifer had been waiting to see if any more air cars pulled into the lot from the direction of the abduction holding site location miles away down the road.

She had done a thorough geographic survey of the surrounding countryside around the holding site. Her HC had a good map reader app. Four roads led to the location from three directions.

A short time later, Jennifer saw a security guard park his old looking air car and lock it, then go into the eatery. The man had come from the direction of the holding site.

Surveillance finished. Jennifer had no intention of entering the restaurant. She was an outsider and would be spotted as such immediately. Jennifer could only guess that many, if not most, of the patrons she had watched enter the diner were working at the holding site. Same with the security guard.

The air car whirred to life, the low hum of the grav gen lifting it up gently. Jennifer steered the air car slowly out into light traffic gaining speed, heading back to Sommerville.

No undue exposure, no silly attempts to ask questions, nothing to pull attention to herself. Jennifer realized that she had just now let out her breath. Her eyes spotted a fast moving security air car growing larger in size in the rear-view mirror. The strobes were not lit.

In the passenger seat were many tools to protect herself from an imminent attack. Jennifer's heart beat a bit faster but not pounding. She had prepared for this eventuality.

The security air car swerved around Jennifer heading for the city, getting smaller and smaller, barreling down the road in front of her.

Yesterday she had followed the air ambulance in a similar situation to D ghetto.

Today she was not going to repeat that tactic. This could be a trap. Simple as that. Instead, Jennifer banked left at a stop crossing. Once on a new trajectory, she called up the map reader to guide her back to D ghetto. But the route she took was an enormous, circuitous bend out and away from Sommerville.

On her way back to D ghetto, Jennifer stopped for food at a quick mart. She bought all the pre-made sandwiches the store had in the cold case, eighteen in all. She filled her arms with the sandwiches and plopped them on the counter as the clerk began scanning them. Jennifer pulled an assortment of plasti bottle beverages from the walk-in, paid for the whole lot and left.

Jennifer spent the rest of the afternoon doing numerous counter surveillance maneuvers in the air car. The countryside was unforgiving in line of sight. Tracking, retracting, turning, feigning, stopping, driving back-and-forth sometimes four times in a row. Jennifer did everything she could to eliminate a tail.

At one point Jennifer came to a wooded forest with a historical marker explaining the significance of the acreage the protected forest represented. She pulled into the air car lot then backed up to the tree line. After waiting 30 minutes, Jennifer pulled out the floater drone. The drone powered up, and she sent it down the single track bike path off into the woods. Casually leaning against the air car, Jennifer studied the screen as though she was communicating back and forth with someone responding to their messages.

She inspected all the bends in the path, finally satisfied no one was hiding in the woods. She then guided the drone out the far side of the forest. Hugging the drone close to the ground, Jennifer followed the contours of the countryside up and over the backside of a wide set of hills. Following the backside of the hills, she popped the drone from cover and zoomed the vid cam back in the direction she had just traveled inspecting the road for anything suspicious.

She repeated the procedure in the direction she was headed just to be sure. The pit stop ended up shedding over two hours before the drone was safely deposited back into Jennifer's air car boot.

It wasn't until well after 6:30 that Jennifer arrived at the spillway underpass in D ghetto. The sun was yet again sagging down past the rim of the spillway wall.

Jennifer powered down the air car and listened to the sound of the quiet interior for a minute. She pulled a water bottle from the cup holder and took a few drinks thinking about what she had to accomplish next. Tipping back the plasti bottle for another drink, her head turned spotting the mural again. In the fading light it was more difficult to see, and so was the additional artwork.

Jennifer had been gone all day executing her foray. During that time someone had added to the drawing. An image of a burning vehicle with exaggerated smoke billowing from the wreckage was inserted at about two o'clock up off of the left shoulder. The air ambulance was tattered and bent with sharp flames beneath the tails of rising black smoke. The representation of this morning's event was about one-fifth the size of the mighty woman's image.

The water bottle stayed paused in mid-gulp against her lips as Jennifer gathered in this stark oddity, failing to comprehend how it appeared so fast and accurately. Jennifer finally admitted to herself that she didn't understand how it portrayed the foray—to her knowledge no one had followed her.

Jennifer returned the water bottle to the cup holder shaking off her confusion with a sniff.

There's no sense fighting this. It is what it is.

By habit, Jennifer remembered to take two pills. She grabbed up the water and washed them down.

She exited the air car carrying an armful of sandwiches to the fire-side chairs. No one was around at the moment. It took three trips before Jennifer had all the food and beverages set down next to the chairs.

Jennifer's HC vibrated. She sat down pulling it to her ear.

"Captain," Linden greeted her.

"Hello, Linden." Jennifer was tired. He could hear it in her voice.

"I've got people here anxious to lend a hand. But you know that already."

Jennifer smiled wearily.

"Tell Ian he's too big to go covert, which is what I'm all about right now."

Ian was already on the line.

Jennifer didn't have to be told.

"You hear that, Ian?"

"I heard you. Still doesn't help my nerves, but I heard you."

"Relax, I think I'm doing okay so far."

There was a long pause.

"I had to ask you to let your friends help you before. Seems like this is getting to be a life-long job for me." Ian had done so during the mission to save Krachy from the hunting resort.

"You don't trust me," Jennifer stated flatly.

"Screw you!" He snapped. Ian was usually very good natured, but in this instance his button had been pressed mightily. "And screw you for thinking—"

Jennifer broke in.

"—Damn, don't get so mad at me."

Ian was silent.

His silence bothered her more than his insults.

"It's only been two days. I want to pull a solid plan around this. I'm being very cautious. Linden has done a good job of setting the ground rules. Right, Linden?" Jennifer asked, trying to petition some help.

"You have, Captain. But things are changing. I've found out more about the scale of what's taking place on-planet. As I'm sure you have already too."

There was no doubt Linden knew her well.

"I am aware of the planet-wide extent. Yes."

Ian cut in harshly.

"—And you think you can handle this alone?"

"No, Ian I do not think that," Jennifer shot back thinking about Darla.

"What then?"

"Look, I've managed to save two lives already. Grant it, both of those lives were mine to save, but I made the right choices. I've managed to find an extremely discreet place to conduct my operation that fell right into my lap because I rescued a woman. So that makes it three lives in the win column. Stop preaching to me about what, then? What, now? Blah, blah."

The rancor Jennifer spit in her reply was easy to muster given that no one had died that wasn't supposed to, which was the only condition that needed to be met to categorize what she had accomplished so far as a win. That condition was her promise, and damn if she wasn't going to fight to keep it.

Ian tried another approach.

"At least let your IA bodyguards break orbit to help you."

"Before we go there, can you please tell me how Jeff is getting along?"

Ian was devious at times. The next voice that spoke proved it.

"My Lord," Dimitri Volodya said.

Jennifer was being ganged up on but she only had herself to blame for that.

"Dimitri, will you please tell me how Jeff is doing?"

As could be expected from her other sworn vassal, Dimitri filled her in.

"Jeffrey was tanked until this morning. The skin over the near full length of the back of his body has re-gened to the point that it's starting to grow on its own. He cannot, however, lie on his back yet. He's still in the mobility bed prone. He's eating but number two is a bit of a challenge, number one, not so much."

"When your plumbing works life is good."

Dimitri heard the smile in her voice. Jennifer was thrilled to hear everything Dimitri said. Not to mention, as her sworn vassal, he was not going to berate her, so this was a safe zone as far as conversations went. Nice.

"Tell Ian that's all I wanted to know."

"Certainly, my Lord."

This is what Jennifer loved about her vassals. They wanted to serve, not change.

"Thank you, Dimitri. You've already been told why I'm here alone."

"Yes I have."

"I know you think I'm strong, and at times that may be true. Most times. But after what nearly happened to Jeff, I decided to approach what I wanted to do a different way."

"I understand as much as anyone, my Lord. I'm from Pinat after all." The warrior cast males from that planet had genetic abilities different from any other planet Jennifer had ever visited. Specifically, the Right Way. This inbred genetic trait allowed Dimitri to change his conscious self to adapt to any type of goal. In essence, Dimitri could change his mind in a way that framed his goals so that he would not deviate from them. All this could be accomplished without conscious thought. Astonishingly, the Right Way could also be focused to repair bodily injuries. At least to an extent, that is.

Jennifer didn't have this innate ability, but what she was trying now was as close as she may ever get. All of this was being attempted to save others she cared about from being hurt.

Ian back on the line, commented sarcastically.

"So I guess I should thank you for not putting me in the line of fire then."

"Ha," Jennifer chuckled. "You're welcome."

"It's good to hear your voice," Ian said seriously.

"You too, Ian. You and I have been at this a long time. I would never take this so far to purposely hurt you."

"I know."

"I know you know, I just wanted you to hear me say it. And before you ask, don't put Carol on the line."

Ian could picture Jennifer's grin.

"She's cagey and a downright pest, Jennifer!"

Jennifer filled Ian in more.

"I just got back from a successful foray that lasted all day. I need to go to the restroom and eat. The restroom part is a bit more challenging than usual. A young woman I rescued is homeless. As are all the people harboring me at the moment."

"Bet they're sharp as lasers. Aren't they?"

Jennifer nodded her head. Ian was spot on.

"Very. They have to be. They've been a huge asset so far. I slept through a covert op they did to supply me with armaments. They even took the initiative to set up something that I've never done before. I didn't even ask for their help. I was floored."

"About what?" Ian asked.

"What?"

"Why were you surprised, Jennifer?"

"I didn't ask for their help. I said that."

"You saved one of their clan. Of course they want to help. I think I can start to feel better about this now. Nice work."

Jennifer knew Ian was procrastinating now. It was hanging in the air thick as mud.

"You need to talk to your husband—soon!"

"Yes. You're right."

"He will not be my friend much longer unless you give me a specific time."

"Two hours. I'll comm him. I promise."

Ian's relief was palpable.

"Thank you."

Ian cut the feed.

Jennifer grabbed a sandwich and beverage noticing that two people were walking her way. She could feel a nice calm smooth over the tension in her body. The medication she used was effective and long lasting. Some shoulder and neck muscles released and her anxiety about the day's events seemed as far away as a dream.

Jennifer didn't want to be rude. With the fast sequence of events so far, she only had a chance to meet Darla. But she had to pee and grab a nap or she might slur her words when she talked with Krachy. Unfortunately, that was sometimes a side effect of her head trauma. It was a bit selfish not to have a meal with her hosts, but if Krachy heard her deficient speech it would only worry him more. She just couldn't do that to him after heading off on this thing without even a check-in beforehand.

Instead, Jennifer motioned for the two women to grab whatever they wanted then hiked back across the spillway toward the air car. She went to the bathroom on the far side of the vehicle then climbed in the passenger side, but kept the door up and open while she ate. Her HC vibrated and she smiled.

"Hi, love." The growing smile felt good on her face.

"Hey," Krachy said. "Couldn't wait."

"I'm glad. Thanks."

"You eating?"

Jennifer chewed but wasn't really tasting much at the moment. The meds made moments like this dreamy for sure.

"Dinner." She pulled her legs into the air car and shut the door, clearing her throat after a swig of water. "That's better. I haven't had much time to myself. But I love it when we're one-on-one, when we come undone. I'm in my air car now. It's dark here."

"You sound great. How do you feel?"

Krachy could always, always make her feel like a woman.

Jennifer didn't even glance out the windows to see if anyone was around.

"I feel good." Her hand dropped over her crotch.

"I miss you. But I know you have to do this. I support you. Always."

Along with all the damn adrenaline over the past two days, to hear the man she loved say something like that made her so horny she nearly gasped when her hand pressed over her privates.

"Shit, I'm gonna bust one if you keep that up," Jennifer cooed.

"Be my guest."

"Oh gosh, I effin' love you. I know I tell you that a lot. It's so good the way you treat me. With you, I can let go."

"Rub one out, sweetie. I'll talk you through it."

"No man has ever made me feel like you do. Remember when you came to me when I needed you that first time?"

Krachy laughed.

"No."

"Bullshit."

"Ian just contacted me. I DID NOT listen in on your comm with him."

"I know. I can sense things like that."

"I couldn't wait to tell you how proud I am of you."

Jennifer swallowed, her eyes tearing up.

"How can you do that?"

"Do what?"

"I'm speechless. You know why I'm here and you love me for it. I'm, I'm just speechless. And here I was scared to tell you."

"No biggie. You'll probably do something like this again. I want to be your hubby for a long time."

"Tell me how long."

"A few months."

Jennifer grinned.

"Yeah, right."

"No really. What you're doing right now will secure you a two month extension—three if you succeed."

Jennifer knew he was teasing.

Krachy said more sternly.

"Just don't take too long to finish. I like having you sleep in the same bed. You're tall as shit."

"You're short as hell."

"You have small boobs."

"You have a nic—"

"—We're still newlyweds. That's not my best feature."

"Wow! Well what is?"

"Un-Un, nope, can't tell you until you get back."

"Major incentive!"

SEVEN

After talking to Krachy, Jennifer slept better than she had in weeks.

A hand on her shoulder roused Jennifer. She stretched her arms over head and turned pulling open her rested eyelids.

It was time.

Darla was looking down at her.

"Early bird and all that stuff." She had ditched the blanket and had on some dirty faded blue trousers and a navy blue long sleeved shirt.

Jennifer rubbed her eyes, then pulled them open wider at the smell of coffee.

Darla held out a styro cup of black coffee, the rim missing small chunks in places.

Jennifer grabbed it.

"How did you know I take it black?"

Darla grunted.

"Get real. No creamer."

Jennifer gathered it in gratefully taking a sip.

"My bad." She got out and stood up.

Darla handed the canister of pepper spray to Jennifer.

"Take this and the key."

Jennifer did.

"Measures is asleep. Go do your thing," Darla instructed and retreated across the spillway to where several of her friends were just starting the morning around a newly built fire.

The time was after 5am. The part of the morning where people were most tired and usually sleeping hard.

Like Laura Measures.

Jennifer finished her coffee, palmed the pepper spray, and stalked off to confront Measures.

Laura Measures' raspy breathing was audible when Jennifer stepped up to the improvised detention cell. Darla and her friends had secured her in an alcove near the crest of the spillway. The squat little four-feet-wide by five-feet-deep crevice housed an old pump valve. The ceramacrete lined niche allowed access to the round turn wheel for some sort of pump long since unused. It had a dura chain-link fence door that prevented unauthorized access. Now it was being used as a cage for Measures. It was secured with an old-fashioned padlock, which Jennifer had the key to.

Measures startled awake with a scared jerk when Jennifer turned the key in the padlock. The prisoner's right eye was still swollen—but it creased open part way in alarm when Jennifer took a threatening step forward after pulling the fence door open on its hinge.

Measures scooted back a feeble few inches and curled herself up tighter into a ball, clearly frightened about the reason Jennifer showed up in the middle of the night.

Jennifer's left arm straightened. Measures spotted the black canister in her hand and pulled in a tight short breath of terror.

Just then Measures caught movement behind Jennifer, coming in low, under her line of sight, creeping up the slanted wall of the spillway. It was GUNNY! The middle-aged man held a laser blade in his right hand that was not alight at the moment.

Measures forced her unnerved confused eyes back to Jennifer, not really sure that GUNNY was going to do what she hoped he would.

Before Measures figured out what she was seeing, GUNNY snapped on the L blade. He shot an arm around Jennifer's throat and pulled her onto the shank, driving it into her back. From the sound of the impact, maybe even seating it in a lung.

Jennifer tensed, dropping the canister by reflex, then wilted to the spillway wall pushing out a long harsh breath on her way down. GUNNY had already extracted the laser blade. He stood over Jennifer's quiet body looking at Measures urgently.

"C'mon, let's go!" GUNNY motioned. He pocketed the weapon.

Measures' fitness helped her shake off the fatigue, disbelief, and gratitude competing to win the battle about what'd just happened. She sprung up and grabbed GUNNY's hand being pulled along behind him.

"Thank you! Thank you, GUNNY!" Measures shot a spooked look back to make sure her tormentor wasn't following.

The two arms dealers ran up over the wall of the spillway pumping their legs hard, then took a left into an alleyway where an air car was parked.

GUNNY arrived at the back door, pulled it up and open fast, then yanked Measures' hand, flinging the jittery escapee into the back. He shut the door then lunged in behind the controls, pushing the throttle hard. More and more distance started to separate Laura Measures from captivity before she felt safe enough to look up from the back seat.

"Stay down!" GUNNY yelled.

Laura did as she was told pressing her cheek into the back seat breathing hard.

"Oh, Laura. You don't know how lucky you are. That woman I just knifed picked up your order yesterday posing as you. I planted a tracker in one of the weapons that led me here." GUNNY pulled himself higher in his seat with the control stick so he could look in the rear-view mirror at Laura's cowering face.

GUNNY shook his head.

Laura started to rise up again.

He snapped.

"Get back down! I just told you that woman got a full order. Her damn ghetto friends might try to use the stuff and take us out! Keep your damn head DOWN!"

Up ahead GUNNY banked hard around a corner. Laura was thrown sideways with a yawp.

"I owe you, I owe you, GUNNY!" Some terror was being replaced with relief in Laura's voice. "That bitch tried to make me tell her who my floater client was. She asked hard! Look at me, just look at me!"

When Laura started to pull herself up so GUNNY could see what Jennifer had done to her eye, GUNNY swung his arm into the back seat and pushed her head back down.

"Stay the hell down! We're not out of this yet!"

GUNNY yanked a turn.

"Why was she pressing so hard?"

"Because I didn't know the end client. I just know how to set up the buy with the end client." The pitch of Laura's strained voice decreased with each word. She was starting to believe that she might just get out of this nightmare in one piece.

"Set up?" GUNNY jerked the controls, the air car lurched around another corner. "What set up?"

Laura braced herself for another banking turn. She exhaled a hysterical laugh, giddy that she was escaping.

"Ha, I didn't tell the bitch because I don't know who comes to the drop."

"What drop?"

Laura's head came up starting to clear the seat.

GUNNY turned and hissed.

"Keep down!" The air car shot around a bend.

Adrenaline sluiced her chest. She licked her lips.

"I have a drop for the client at a church on Abalong. I don't know who picks up the goods. I just know how to make the church bell chime 10 times at 11."

"You're crafty, Laura. What, you make the client go into a confessional?"

"No, the cemetery 'round back. One of the benches is hollow." She giggled nervously, confident she was going to be free in a few minutes.

When Laura's confidence about that freedom pulled her chin above the seats, she got a good look out the front windshield.

Laura wasn't processing the person standing with hands on hips framed in the headlamps until the air car slowed to a stop.

Jennifer Bane narrowed her eyes, a thin smile fringing her mouth.

Laura Measures' eyelids bolted apart in alarm. The first panicked words out of her mouth had to get past a fear-constricted gurgle in her throat.

"She's dead! You killed her! She's dead!"

GUNNY jumped out of the air car as Laura Measures screamed in disbelief from the back seat curling herself into a tight ball against the door trembling.

"No, I saw you kill her, I saw it! No! You killed her, GUNNY! You did!"

Darla handed Jennifer a flechette rifle then Jennifer came around to the driver door aiming it at the horror-stricken woman cowering in the back seat.

"Get out, Laura. Play time is over."

While Laura Measures was returned to her makeshift cell, GUNNY got paid for services rendered. Before he went on his way, he told Jennifer and Darla everything Measures spilled. Jennifer watched GUNNY's air car pick up speed heading out of D ghetto, then turned to Darla.

"The church shouldn't be hard to find," Jennifer commented offhand, reaching a hand back to rub the impact spot of the laser blade hilt.

Darla's pupils flared.

"So was I right?"

Jennifer lifted her chin.

"Right about what?"

"That this thing is playing out different than you thought."

Jennifer's head jerked side-to-side matter of factly.

"Can't argue with you there. I would have never thought of using GUNNY to fool Measures like that. He snapped the blade on, off, then back on so fast it looked like he rammed it up into my back. From Measures' point of view it must have looked pretty real."

"Obviously." Darla raised an eyebrow. "Your body shielded the farce."

Jennifer rubbed at the sore spot on her back again.

"The hilt smacked me good, though. Hurt."

"You get what you pay for. Correction: We got what Measures paid for—again. I gave GUNNY the same amount I paid for the order. That makes three payments of the same amount. Measures' bank account is draining fast."

"I think I know what to do with the intel he gave us," Jennifer reasoned.

"Sounds like a dead drop to me."

Jennifer pulled her brows together in a frown.

"How do you know about stuff like tha—?" She caught the slip. "Sorry, I know you're not dense."

"I'd say we've made a reliable consort out of GUNNY. Wouldn't you?"

"I didn't do that, Darla. That was all you. And yes, I'd say his greed can definitely be counted on now. At least until Measures' bank balance runs dry." Jennifer tugged at an earlobe.

"What, Jennifer?"

"You've done so much for me I hate to ask."

"Ask what?"

"It's, it's jus—" Jennifer stammered.

"What already?"

Jennifer's words came out in a rush.

"I have this friend, a man that's watched my back like forever, and he's worried sick about what I'm doing." She gathered herself, talking slower. "Think you could comm my First Officer Ian McKivey and chat with him? It'd be a big help."

Darla smile was gentle.

"Sure."

"Thank you—for everything."

***

This was a time Jennifer liked, when she was working a problem and she was truly *alone* on a stakeout. Most people that were usually around her couldn't handle a solitude where they couldn't call someone for backup. But when she had involved others in her maneuverings to find out the truth, or to aid and assist, people got hurt.

Since I really am the captain of my own privateer team again maybe I should just approach every mission like I am now. I'm the boss aren't I?

The absurd, but now archived thought, pulled her eye back from staring through the sniper scope. *I'm going to mull that idea over again after tucking it away for further consideration. Absurd? Maybe. Attainable? Hmmmm...We'll see.* Jennifer pictured opening a drawer and stashing this desire inside before closing, but not locking, the chamber.

The flechette rifle beside her on the rooftop was considered a pre-defined kit configured for combat. This is what GUNNY had provided as part of the order delivered to Darla. The rifle included three components: a simple length-adjustable buttstock, adjusted now to Jennifer's longer than average arms, a shortened hand guard grip small enough for her petite hand, and a telescopic sight. The sight was removed. It had an integrated illuminated dot that could, at close range, therefore be used like a conventional red-dot. The sight came standard with 1X to 9X magnification and a built-in dart drop compensation range adjustment. The scope could be adjusted from 100 to over 1,400 yards.

It was lighter than the flechette rifle kit Jennifer had brought with her and used during the firefight to rescue Darla.

Even the scope was flitty, which made the several long hours Jennifer had held it up to her eye easier to accomplish.

Jennifer looked down at Laura Measures' hand comp beside her on the roof. The music app was pulled up to the song, "Abalong Church." The chrono in the upper right corner read 10:59. She depressed the volume toggle on the side of the HC so she could hear the music. This was the third time she had listened to the song because it played on the hour.

When the chrono turned to 11:00, her eyes lifted from the screen to the church steeple over two-hundred yards away from her hide. The digitally recorded music inside the thin rising white triangular steeple atop the church began playing. The soft soothing tune that emanated out through the angled vents surrounding the triangular spire also played on the HC.

Jennifer had found the right church. And, equally as important, a means by which she could control the music and chimes in the spire atop the church.

At the conclusion of the short Abalong Church song snippet, the digital bell chimes rang eleven times.

Jennifer could control the number of times the bell chimed inside the steeple with the hand comp. The Abalong Church song was replaced by "Chimes," a song that mirrored the eleven pings inside the spire.

Jennifer did not alter the number of chimes played.

Laura Measures' HC saved the date/time history of songs played in its memory. Today was Tuesday on the planet Beltina. The last time "Chimes" had played was last Thursday. Therefore, Laura Measures had called for the dead drop behind the church to be accessed sometime after last Thursday.

Jennifer could not see the full view of the small fenced-in cemetery behind the church from her current hide atop the building she was on. The angle was not good. A closer, hands-on inspection, preferably at night, would need to be done to determine which hollow bench had been used for the drop with Measures' exploding floater drone client.

A nagging thought tugged at the periphery of Jennifer's stakeout foray: *Why had Laura Measures returned from off-planet right after the exploding floater injured Jeffrey? I interrogated her very hard and am convinced she did not know who she sold it to. I also had the living daylights deftly removed from her terrified chest during the mock rescue by GUNNY. Laura did not know who her client was. Maybe I'll need to ask her why she had just come home dirt-side.*

Jennifer then thought about her vassal Dimitri, specifically, about his ability to genetically focus his thoughts on the task at hand. Linden had set the stage for her to emulate this special skill. The directive Linden used to pull her focus back to safety was: *Back off, back off! Abort, Captain.*

Simple but profound, Jennifer thought as she gathered up her stakeout kit and retreated cautiously through the rooftop door down the steps.

On the basement level, not ground level, Jennifer crawled under the stairs into the dark dirty alcove the slanted nook provided. She rested her sore back against the rough cerama-crete wall listening and waiting. Jennifer was not tired having slept restfully. She made it a point not to take her meds. They dulled her mental acuity. Her breathing centered, Jennifer sat and listened for any sign of danger for a full two hours. The hardest part was keeping her mind clear of the crisp images of death she had caused since coming dirt-side. Again she thought of Dimitri and his genetically pre-determined ability to push aside such distractions. Her vassal was with her and he didn't even know it.

Jennifer was fiercely determined not to expose Darla and her friends to harm. In the same light, she was committed to unpredictability in her actions. Routine and complacency were dangerous. Therefore, hours later, when Jennifer was satisfied no one was following her, she exited the building on the ground level and hurried back to her air car. She carried the combat rifle kit in an inconspicuous large duffle, not a gun case. Jennifer guided the air car out of Sommerville on an entirely new trajectory.

By the time Jennifer executed an exhaustive counter surveillance journey ending under the spillway, it was nearly 7:30 in the evening. Jennifer's anxiety about being discovered was replaced by worry when she was told that Darla was having a drug withdrawal episode.

Jennifer hastily went off in search of her new friend. Apparently Darla wanted to be alone when the symptoms erupted. Jennifer didn't care what Darla wanted—friends helped friends.

As Jennifer left the group of people huddled by the fire, she couldn't help but notice the added mural scene depicting the faux escape. A thin bright orange laser blade rose from the ground behind her image. Jennifer's face was defiant in the face of adversity. The small vignette had been added to the drawing at the 10 o'clock position this time.

Darla's trembling eyes parted when the touch on her forehead pulled her cheek against Jennifer Bane's breast. Darla was hot with fever. Jennifer could tell that she was chilled, so she began rubbing her arms.

Darla's eye whites rolled up into her head, and for a split second, Jennifer thought her young friend was going to expire right in her arms.

Jennifer dabbed at her face with the dirty blanket hem Darla had wrapped around herself. She soothed, rocking the sick helpless girl back-and-forth for a few minutes before pushing the opening of an upturned water bottle to her quivering lips.

Darla's eyes opened registering moisture at the touch on her lips. Her dehydrated body pulled strained gulps of liquid into her parched throat by reflex. Jennifer pushed a yellow tab of the anti-nausea medication Zofran into the stream pulsing down her throat. She kept the pills with her out of necessity just like her head meds.

EIGHT

"Why you pursue something is equally as important as *what* you pursue, Jennifer,"

Ochula Kozlov advised a confused Jennifer Bane via the hand comp pulled to her ear.

Jennifer had just picked up the vibrating HC from the driver seat in her air car. Her groggy head was fuzzy, barely recognizing the voice on the other end.

Darla's symptoms had lessened overnight after Jennifer kept forcing her to drink liquids to prevent dehydration. Two Z tabs staggered at the appropriate time intervals helped as well. Jennifer was very familiar with the drug having used it reduce nausea many times. Jennifer spent a long night with Darla helping her through her withdrawal sickness. She only got to sleep a few hours ago.

Jennifer pulled the reclined seat upright sitting straighter. She threw a hand over her eyes to deaden the sunshine. The sun was way up over the spillway wall. *Must be afternoon. Maybe I slept longer than I thought?*

"Ochula?" She asked befuddled.

Commander Ochula Kozlov was the head of the military on her home planet of Markem. Jennifer had worked with him when she brokered a truce between Markem and Beltina. They'd stayed in touch and remained friends but she had not seen or heard from him in quite a while. Krachy had served with Ochula when he was part of the Markem military. They were good friends and comrades. Krachy had even wanted Ochula to be the best man at their wedding, but Ochula couldn't break free from his responsibilities on Markem at the time.

"Fair warning: I'm coming to see you. Don't shoot!" He ordered.

It WAS him!

"Ochula, what are you talking about? You're here? What?! Wait a minute..!" Jennifer squinted her eyes against the piercing sun. She sniffed and swallowed trying to process Ochula's statement.

A knuckle rapped on the driver side window a few times startling Jennifer. The man was tall and sturdy. When he shifted his body to one side, he blocked the bright rays of sun penetrating Jennifer's skull allowing her to focus on his face as he leaned down.

Jennifer swallowed.

Ochula Kozlov pulled the door up and open then jumped in the driver seat turning towards her.

"Good afternoon," he jibbed. "You look like hell, Bane. Being homeless doesn't seem to agree with your beauty sleep."

Jennifer paled, speechless.

"Good to see you too…"

"—I," Jennifer sputtered.

Ochula turned reaching out the door for something on the ground. He pulled a small backpack into his lap, unzipped it, and shot his hand inside digging for something. He pulled it out, holding it in one hand.

"I've been watching you since I picked up your image in the headlamps of that air car with the terrified woman in the back," Ochula explained, gripping an auto monocular. "You were gone all day yesterday. I didn't want to spook your friends by approaching until you were around, so I waited until you crawled back into your air car this morning to sleep. Your friend looked really sick. I hope she's okay." His lips turned down.

"You've been watching me?"

"Since early yesterday."

The smile on her lips rose to her eyes.

Ochula's brown eyes were playful.

"You're slipping, Jennifer." He shook his head once. "Your evasion techniques left out a hard target search of the immediate area around the spillway. Remember," he instructed like a fifth-grade teacher, "a plant can be inside your perimeter before you even start. Always do a routine patrol of your immediate surroundings."

Jennifer took in an admiring breath.

"I'm glad it was you watching me."

Ochula shoved the monocular back in the pack and zipped it shut with a pull. He looked at Jennifer waiting.

She saw the look on his face.

"What?"

"You've made an impression here." Ochula turned and scanned the immediate vicinity around the air car his eyes landing on the mural on the other side of the spillway. Not looking at Jennifer he commented, "They admire you." He turned back to her.

Jennifer looked past Ochula taking in the mural for a moment, then focused on his face.

"I admire them too. I'm just glad my friend Darla made it through the night."

"I can't tell you how tough it was not to come and help."

Jennifer's face held a touch of a smile.

"You couldn't do more than me. Besides, she's a strong woman...a fighter."

"Glad to hear it."

"These people have changed the way I look at things. Their whole life is based on compassion, not fear. They have so little control over what happens to them, they don't expend energy worrying about it. I worry about way too much. That's the main reason I'm here now."

"Protecting?"

Jennifer's brows lifted.

"Not a bad thing though, right?"

"No. There another reason?"

Jennifer didn't answer. She studied Ochula's face looking for signs of judgement. There weren't any, or were there?

"I shouldn't be out for revenge too. That's what you're saying?"

"I realize stuff like that is important to you."

"That's not an answer."

"I'm not here to judge, Jennifer, if that's what you're thinking."

"How long you been rogue?"

"Six days."

Jennifer's eyes widened.

"If you've been covert that long then you've had to have been dirt-side longer than that. A guy with your job doesn't just visit Beltina without being noticed."

"You're right. I came to meet with Lad Blanconales over a week ago."

"Why didn't the president of Markem come?"

"The guy's sick so I came as his proxy. Anyway, Blanconales conveniently forgot to mention the planet-wide breakdown in public trust. I didn't press him about it. Instead I let him remind me about how his planet still has a decided military advantage over my planet."

"The Receiver."

"Yes, the Receiver." Ochula's brows peaked. "The president has regularly scheduled meetings, more like beat downs, with Blanconales. He puts us in our place and we promise to be a respectful cease-fire partner. He likes to remind us of our role as a subordinate. We don't push back. We can't. The existence of the Receiver really does keep us in line. Its capabilities make Beltina's military superiority absolute. We know it and Blanconales knows it. Things are tenuous but stable between his planet and ours." Ochula shrugged a big shoulder. "However, him not mentioning the abductions, and his silly assumption that I wouldn't know about them, caused me to act."

Jennifer cocked her head.

"I used a body double. Actually, I've been using one for years when the need arises. I had my look-alike leave after the meetings and I stayed."

"To find out what's really happening." Jennifer's eyes were quizzical.

"To find out what's really happening," Ochula agreed. "I've learned a lot staying in the shadows. I've been conducting recon patrols outward from my own base of operation further east. About two miles from here. I've been blending in with the street people, keeping to myself. It's amazing how friendly these people are to others."

"Why did you pick Sommerville and not the capital?"

"Less area to cover, and it's not far from the capital. Since the abductions are planet-wide, I figured Sommerville was as good a place to start as any. Then two days ago I spotted a smoke plume west of here that turned out to be an attack on an air ambulance and firetruck. That got me more curious. And it confirmed something I hadn't witnessed until then—firefighters are taking people too."

"I did that." Jennifer admitted reluctantly, not happy to take credit.

Ochula dipped his head once, pulling his lips into a fine line of support.

Jennifer loved her friend for that.

"I wanted to see if firefighters were a part of all this. Plus it took another one of their teams off the board." Then she dropped the bomb. "The prime minister wants to integrate the Insect Alien Collective into Beltan society. Jeffrey told me that Blanconales asked for me to be the go-between. Minutes after that, a drone tried to take me out. Jeffrey and my two IA body guards shielded me from the blast. Jeffrey was hurt bad."

"Is he going to be okay?"

"I think so."

"Someone doesn't want the IAs to be assimilated," Ochula asserted.

"It would appear so."

"How do the abductions further that goal?"

"Hostages for leverage?" Jennifer guessed.

"Maybe." Ochula considered it further. "The key is who's in charge, or *what's* in charge."

"I know the address of one location being used to house hostages…If that's what they really are. I interrogated an EMT."

Ochula could only imagine what Jennifer did with the person afterwards.

Jennifer saw it on his face.

"I didn't kill the person," she spat quickly.

"Is the woman I saw that was scared out of her mind the EMT?" Ochula asked referring to Laura Measures.

"No. I let the EMT go with a warning. The woman you saw is the arms dealer that sold the floater to the assassin that tried to kill me. The woman doesn't know the buyer but did tell me how the buyer places orders. That's what I was doing yesterday. I found out where the dead drop is located for the exchange."

"Seems like we've been working the problem from different sides, Jennifer."

Jennifer let out a breath of relief.

"It is good to see you, Ochula. Darla and her friends have risked a lot helping me."

Ochula knew what she meant.

"You don't want to stay here?"

"I do know that I'm scared to get too close to the abduction holding site, and bring down a world of hurt on myself and Darla's people if I screw up."

Ochula wrinkled his nose.

"The IAs are telepaths."

"That small fact has not escaped me," Jennifer acknowledged seriously.

"If Insect Aliens are the end customer, however unlikely that may be, then they could read your mind before you get close to the dead drop."

"This thing could blow up real fast, Ochula."

Ochula swallowed, pressing his lips together.

"I could go in your place. Any telepaths would be focused on you, not me. Wearing a brain coat would help too. An effective skull cap should prevent intrusion, mind monitoring."

Jennifer pulled in a breath, hesitating.

"What?" Ochula asked. "You don't think I can handle it?"

"That's a dumb question."

"What then?"

"You're pressing me to make a decision I'm not ready to make!" Jennifer huffed more loudly than she intended. "You just got here, and now you want me to send you in like a pawn to get clipped. Stop that!"

Ochula had known Jennifer a long time. He had always admired how truthful she was. She never pulled punches. That's one of the most endearing traits he liked about his friend. No one on his staff was *filterless* like her.

"What's with the shit-eating grin?" Jennifer's anger ticked up another notch.

"I'm touched that you care."

Jennifer scrunched a cheek.

"You're not gonna guilt me into something damn it! I just woke up." She glanced out the back of the air car. "I haven't even checked on my friend Darla yet."

"Should I go with you or leave?" Ochula asked thoughtfully.

"I'm sure the others have seen you by now. What I don't want to do is flaunt my perceived status over them. I don't want them to think that I can do anything I want or bring anyone into their camp without permission. I'm already unsettled that they drew a homage to me on that wall. Them doing that makes me even more frightened about letting them down." Jennifer shook her head uncomfortably.

"Here." Ochula pulled out his hand comp, touched the screen a few times, then pressed it to Jennifer's HC in her hand. It chirped. "That's my contact info. I'll leave the way I came. Let me know when you're ready to talk more." He climbed out of the air car then outstretched a hand on the roof so he could look down at Jennifer. "Take your time. I'd never rush you. You know that." He turned, pulling the backpack on, and quickly hiked over the stream bounding up the spillway wall east out of sight.

Jennifer sat watching the back of Ochula's head disappear over the rim of the spillway. *He came here on his own,* she reasoned. *I didn't ask, so that means I'm not responsible, right?*

Just then Jennifer heard the faint sound of music echoing off the walls of the spillway. She sensed that the music was coming from behind her. She pushed her door open climbing out. The sound pulled her along past the back of the air car and under the bridge. The volume began to increase as she navigated the wide bend at the base of the spillway in the direction of Laura Measures' temporary detention cell high atop the wall.

Jennifer walked along the bottom of the slanted wall following the music until she rounded the long bend leading to Measures' fenced-in cage. On the floor of the wide spillway were several rows of Darla's friends. They had found a spot where the channel of flowing water arched off toward the opposite wall of the spillway giving them enough room to assemble.

Darla was seated about a third of the way up the sloped wall watching her friends. Jennifer glanced up at the spillway rim. Laura Measures was sitting in her cell with both hands pulling her face against the chain-link fence, fingers gripping through the holes, watching the performance below.

Jennifer stopped for a moment returning her curious eyes to what had to be a *flash mob.*

The music was being broadcast through a tattered speaker sitting on the ground next to the creek channel.

Jennifer hiked up the wall stopping next to Darla. When Darla looked up at her, it brought a wide smile her face.

"Hey, sit with me. Watch," Darla urged, reaching out to grab Jennifer's hand.

Jennifer let herself be pulled down next to Darla. Both women turned to watch the choreographed dance below.

♫ .....*We're lost in music....Caught in a trap.....No turning back....We're lost in music....*♫

The smooth melody of the song pulled the dancers along in unison. The joy evident in their faces ignited an answering smile on Jennifer's face as she watched.

♫ .....*Responsibility, to me is a tragedy.....I'll get a job some other time, uh-huh.....Give me the melody.....That's all that I ever need.....The music is my salvation!.....*♫

The dancers' arms flailed into the sky. They whirled around and seemed to whoop their happiness at Darla as all of their eyes locked onto her in a fleeting expression of joy.

Darla turned to Jennifer appreciatively.

"They're thrilled I'm alive."

Jennifer returned her look.

"Me too."

As soon as the flash mob peaked, the music stopped, Darla's friends already dispersing to go about their day.

NINE

Jennifer's hand comp trilled. She pulled it to her ear.

"I spotted something," Ochula Kozlov warned. Jennifer had taken the time to brush her teeth using some bottled water and change clothes after speaking with Darla. Now she stood looking down into the open boot of her air car having put away her suitcase.

She had sensed this would happen. After the two attacks on the faux first responders, her handiwork was bound to bring attention.

"Advanced scouts?" Jennifer asked. "I think they're just after me, not you."

"Most likely. A solitary air bike. I've caught her doing what looks like a recon patrol a mile-and-a-half east of you. She's passed by my location three times now. Given this is a desolate part of town, I'm wondering why she keeps doing a clockwise loop of the same area. The air bike looks too new to belong to anyone around here," Ochula added.

"I can't let her widen her search and catch sight of me. I have to assume they know what I look like. How they know doesn't matter right now," Jennifer explained having already decided what to do next. "I'm coming to you," she asserted.

Jennifer brought up the map reader app on her HC; before she could ask, Ochula confirmed.

"I just sent you my location."

"I see it, Ochula. Flag me down like you're looking for a handout, maybe hitching a ride," Jennifer instructed.

"Copy that."

Jennifer pulled out the selection of armaments she would need placing them in the back seat. It took several trips before she had collected what she needed. Finally finished, she shut the boot, climbed behind the controls, and surged the air car out from under the bridge heading east.

Jennifer drove the short distance to the street Ochula was on. She was two turns from his location when she finally admitted to herself that she was being too cautious. Instead of taking the fight to the enemy, the enemy was bringing the fight to her. The disdain at the thought registered in a hard, chilling glare on Jennifer's face.

She banked the air car around the last corner spotting her friend.

Ochula seemed to blend in with the group of homeless people up ahead, keeping sullenly to himself as he tucked his backpack tightly under an arm. He was tall next to the other people and dressed in dark multi-pocket trousers with a brown long sleeved flannel shirt. Ochula pulled his look up. He scanned the street spotting Jennifer decelerating as she approached the stop crossing. He ran over in front of Jennifer's slowing air car causing her to hit the brake to avoid hitting him. He pulled out a dirty rag and bottled water from his pack sloshing a healthy splash on the driver-side windshield. With the rag he started cleaning the wet spot. After a dozen or so swipes, he shuffled to the driver window expecting a tip for his meager service.

Jennifer lowered the auto window and faked touching her HC to his to exchange creds. The two talked for a moment for the benefit of their audience.

While play acting with what seemed to be a homeless vagrant, Jennifer's eyes danced to the rear-view mirror. The woman on the air bike had just pulled around the corner behind her decelerating to a stop, watching.

Ochula's body was half-turned with his left hip resting against the air car. He spotted the sentry stop down the block.

"She's talking, moving her mouth, which means she's in communication with the rest of her team," Ochula explained. "They've got you cold. But they don't know you know they're on to you. And they don't know I'm on your team."

Jennifer's knuckles whitened on the controls despite herself. She was more upset with herself for letting this happen than fearful of the scout and her team. She looked up at Ochula.

"Knowledge is power," Jennifer declared. "We'll just pull the scout and her team into a trap." She shared a conspiratorial wink with him.

Ochula turned and rounded the front of the air car coming around to jump in the passenger side. He pulled the door open and climbed in. The door closed.

Jennifer accelerated through the next block remembering a spot out in the countryside that would work for her intended purposes—purposes *plural*. She was going to eliminate the black bag team dogging her. That was a given. She was also going correct her mistake and push this fight to the enemy. They'd never expect that, which is exactly why she intended to do it.

She worked the controls steering the air car through the suburbs.

Ochula shifted in his seat, sneaking a peek at what was in the back seat, his eyes widening.

"This is a bit overkill, isn't it?" He asked half-heartedly. The glimpse at the armaments told Ochula that Jennifer had MUCH more planned than just eliminating the hit team following her.

Jennifer shook her head.

"Not for what I have in mind." Her lips tightened into a bloodless line. "We've got one set of eyes on us with a commo. We have to assume there's also a backup, because these people aren't stupid." Jennifer glanced at the side mirror, banking the air car around another corner. "If we put down the one tailing us, her backup calls the rest of the team and they know the game is up. Then the rest of the team drops like a hammer. This air car can't take a pounding."

Ochula agreed.

"Just because I haven't spotted the air bike backup, doesn't mean it's not there." It wasn't a question, just an admission.

"Two scouts and a hit team," she confirmed.

Jennifer relaxed her grip on the controls running over her battle plan behind watchful eyes.

"And?" Ochula prodded.

Jennifer's smile was not friendly.

"My chief security officer said something that made me think—*twofer*. Our first step is to take out the bag team. Second step is to take the fight to the enemy and shake the tree. I'm tired of going in the side door on this mess. I'm even more tired of people trying to kill me. The more time I take to find out who's behind all this, the more time it gives them to harm someone close to me. I'm finished effin' around, Ochula."

Ochula looked at the weapons behind him briefly.

"I gathered."

"Besides, you're here now. I didn't have backup before, real backup. Now I do. You okay with that? I don't want to put you in the middle of something you don't want to be wrangled into in the first place."

Ochula maintained eye contact with Jennifer. His menacing look said it all.

"We need to get to the bottom of this." His head dipped once. "I'm in."

Jennifer slowed forcing the woman on the air bike to hang back more. She made one, two, then a third turn looking for the right spot up ahead. There, at the next stop crossing, was a row of hedges on the right. The hedges were thick, angling in from the right following the sidewalk on the cross street. Once she made the right turn, the hedges would shield her air car briefly as she rounded the bend. That would give Ochula enough time.

Jennifer instructed, "Grab the floater behind you. We're going to use it."

Ochula did as he was told. The sturdy floater rested in his lap.

"Where's the controller?" He asked.

Jennifer motioned with a jerk of her head.

"The hand comp between the console."

Ochula pulled the HC to his face fingering the screen. The floater whirred to life lifting a few inches off his lap.

Jennifer slowed to a near stop at the stop crossing.

"Toss it out your window when I turn right."

Ochula thumbed the auto window down as Jennifer eased the air car around the corner. He grabbed the floater with his free hand and flung it at the hedgerow. The arrowhead-shaped drone guided itself into the branches and leaves burrowing into the hedge half-way. Ochula pressed at the on-screen controller hovering the floater where it was.

Jennifer picked up speed so that when the scout came around the same corner she would have to accelerate in the next block to keep her in sight. Chances are she'd be too focused on catching up with Jennifer to notice the floater half submerged in the leafy thicket.

The woman made the right turn, pushing up the throttle on her air bike to keep Jennifer in sight.

Jennifer headed out of town into the countryside. She looked over at Ochula.

"She didn't spot the floater."

Before she could explain further, Ochula started.

"—I get it. I'll fly the drone up high and center the biker." He studied the hand comp finding the correct feature on the small screen. "Got it. I increased the altitude to over seven hundred feet and hit the Point of Interest feature." His eyes squinted. "POI has the air bike centered in the vid now. I see her following us."

Jennifer was into the countryside now. There was much less cover for the air bike to follow without being spotted. She knew what was going to happen soon. *The second scout will take over*, she reasoned.

While waiting for the leapfrog maneuver she knew would happen shortly, Jennifer filled Ochula in.

"The scout following us is going to drop out. The second scout will be up ahead somewhere. Probably parked on a side road. The Drop Out will comm ahead and tell Leap Frog that we're headed his way."

Ochula listened intently. He had known Jennifer a long time and worked with her in much more dangerous situations than what the two of them found themselves in now. He knew what she was capable of. He also recognized the firestorm behind her eyes. He'd seen it before, and each time he had, the people that posed a threat stopped doing so in short order. *Just like today,* he thought to himself.

"We're going to stop at a diner," Jennifer continued. "I spotted it the other day. It's over ten miles from where the people being abducted are being held. Attached to the eatery is a small air car repair shop. I'm going to—"

Ochula stopped her with a raised hand.

"—Drop Out is pulling off, just made a turn on a side road."

Jennifer's eyes flicked to the mirror.

"I see it."

"I'll fly the floater past us to scan the road ahead." His fingers danced on the screen.

Jennifer's grip on the controls loosened a bit.

"Okay, Leap Frog should show up soon. He'll probably pull out ahead of us then slow and let us overtake him."

While they waited for the Leap Frog to engage, Jennifer clarified.

"I'm going to make a show of giving you some creds so you can go into the diner for a bite to eat. I can't go inside. Too risky. When I staked out the restaurant the other day I saw a lot of people go in that came from the direction of the holding site. Instead I'm going to take up position in the repair shop. I'll set something up. Leap Frog won't make his move until his backup is close."

Just then Ochula's eyes widened. He lifted them from the screen nodding.

"Look there." He motioned with his eyes.

Jennifer spotted Leap Frog pull out from a side road on the right. The scout was easy to see.

"How far back will his backup be?" Ochula asked not pulling his eyes from the threat ahead.

"About ten minutes back, maybe less—" Jennifer noticed Leap Frog slowing *her* air bike ahead. The scout was another woman. Oncoming traffic was light. Jennifer pulled out and surged past the slowing air bike pulling back over into slot one. She glanced in the mirror. Leap Frog was hanging back losing speed.

Ochula touched the hand comp screen.

"I've got her pinned with POI. How far until the diner?"

"Just ahead, you see it?"

Ochula looked out the windshield spotting the restaurant/ repair shop in the distance.

"Yeah—" Ochula cut off what he was about to say.

"What?"

"Leap Frog just laid her air bike down." His eyes studied the small screen. "Cloud of dust on the shoulder. Looks like she wiped out," Ochula stated incredulously.

Jennifer shook her head.

"No way, no way she wiped out. It's a ploy, Ochula. She knows there's a repair shop up ahead. She also knows that's about the only thing on this road. Leap Frog is taking a calculated risk that we're going to stop at the eatery."

Jennifer's head turned slowly, her sinister leer nasty.

"Let's not disappoint her."

Jennifer pulled into the air car lot at the restaurant/repair shop and cut the grav gen. She backed into an open spot between other air cars on the right. About three minutes later Jennifer spotted Leap Frog steering the damaged air bike along the shoulder of the road toward them. She was pushing it as though it was damaged.

Jennifer looked over at Ochula.

"Like we discussed, Ochula. Meet me at rendezvous point one. If I don't show, go to the backup location."

Ochula started to say something before exiting the air car.

"—Trust me. I can handle this," Jennifer assured him.

He knew what she meant. Instead of challenging her, he jumped out of the air car waiting for her to exit and meet him in front of the hood.

Jennifer climbed out and came around the front of the air car. Leap Frog was less than fifty yards down the road steering the air bike. The woman's shoulders sagged from the effort it took to push the landing gear wheels along the dusty shoulder. All air bikes had small emergency landing wheels that could be extended to maneuver the air bike if the grav gen failed.

Jennifer pushed her HC against Ochula's. He made a show of smiling a thanks for the creds. He turned and strode over to the cafe entrance going in. Jennifer walked head down into the repair shop garage.

The repair shop owner was standing to one side of the garage watching Jennifer enter.

"Got a cold drink for a lady?" Jennifer locked eyes with the old man.

The elderly guy rubbed his hands on a rag then pointed to the cooler against the left wall.

"Help yourself."

Jennifer lifted the lid on the low bottle cooler pulling out a beverage, pulled back the tab, then took a sip. She pushed her HC to the scan pad on the side of the cabinet; it pinged. She turned and rested her rump on the closed lid watching Leap Frog cross the air car lot toward the garage.

Leap Frog nodded to Jennifer and brought the air bike to a halt resting it on its auto kickstand.

"Ouch," Jennifer said sympathetically.

"Thankfully, not too much damage," Leap Frog replied honestly. "Luckily it wasn't a long walk. Any more drinks in that cooler?"

"A full cooler," Jennifer answered. "Grav gen crapped out. I don't think he has too many spares in here." She looked at the old man watching the two women. "Do you?"

"I can take a look. May not need to be replaced," he answered.

Leap Frog removed her helmet hanging it off the handlebar.

Jennifer scooted off the cooler and pulled the lid up.

"Help yourself."

Leap Frog moved to the cooler bending down to grab a drink.

Jennifer smacked a fist into the woman's kidney. The blow laced the scout's side with liquid flame dropping the woman to her knees. The cooler lid slammed down like an anvil onto her forearm snapping bone.

Leap Frog squealed when she felt the muzzle of Jennifer's laser pistol pressed into the soft tissue under her jaw.

"Relax," Jennifer ordered. "Using two fingers only, give me your LP and laser blade you have hidden."

"How?" The woman gasped, pushing the word past the scalding pain in her arm.

"If I could track your other scout, I can see an amateur like you packing heat on her legs," Jennifer snarled.

The repair shop owner watched the drama going down.

"Well, it certainly does look like she tried to rob me," the man said.

Jennifer eyed the owner confidently.

"I'd keep that L pistol handy," she advised him. The quick exchange convinced Leap Frog that Jennifer had found a willing confederate in the shop owner. "This bitch's friends will be by, and there will be conflict."

The grizzled old man nodded numbly.

"I'd listen to this woman, chickie. She somehow knew I had a laser pistol stuffed in the belt on my back. She's either psychic, or she's killed more people than you've seen in your lifetime."

Leap Frog grunted pulling her L pistol and L blade from concealed holsters on each leg with her good arm. The two weapons clattered to the floor.

"How do you know the old man isn't going to hurt you?" Leap Frog asked.

The old man looked at Leap Frog and sighed.

"Look at this dive. The only thing worth taking are the drinks in that cooler, and she paid for that. What's she gonna shoot me for?"

"Welcome to the big leagues," Jennifer said to Leap Frog, dragging her toward the rickety restroom door in the corner of the shop. Leap Frog cradled her arm and skid pushed her heels into the dirty garage floor trying to help herself along as Jennifer yanked her by the back of the collar.

It only took a few moments for Jennifer to remove the riding jacket and find Leap Frog's sub-vocal microphone and ear-bud. Using a few plasti tie wraps, Jennifer bound the woman to the exposed pipe next to the small sink. She left the scout in the dark behind the closed door.

"You'd best stay inside," Jennifer suggested to the shop owner, shrugging on the riding jacket then reaching for the air bike helmet shoving it on. "I'll keep most of the drama outside—."

Just then an air van banked hard entering the air car lot. A blur of movement snaked down out of the sky spearing right down through the top of the van. The floater drone detonated violently. The metal walls of the van bubbled and deformed radiating outward in a sizzling burst of incendiary might.

Jennifer dove atop the old man. She screamed at the top of her lungs reflexively—her body somehow remembering to protect her head from the blast wave. The two of them were far enough away that the boil of heat reflected off the ground then upward. Heat seared her exposed side. The riding jacket helped her torso escape harm. The helmet protected her melon. Her right leg was not so fortunate. Shards of flying debris stitched through the fabric in a few places drawing blood.

Jennifer respected Ochula for using the floater like a kamikaze. He had just saved her life from the black bag team.

TEN

The old man looked up into Jennifer's eyes coyly.

"That's not my L pistol diggin' into your hip."

"I know," Jennifer smiled, glad they were both alive. "You're happy to see me, aren't you?"

"I don't get many women grinding me to the ground. Especially ones that just saved my life."

Jennifer could hear fine. The helmet spared her ears. She raised an eyebrow.

"Girthy," she commented.

"I've been sportin' wood since you smashed that chickie's arm. You noticed?" He asked hopefully.

Jennifer climbed off the cagey old gent standing.

"I did," she admitted, then fingered her wedding band with a thumb, jiggling it up-and-down a few times for him to see.

"Lucky man."

The old man just laid there smiling. He interlocked his hands behind his head getting comfortable.

Jennifer offered her outstretched hand to him.

He shook his head.

"Nah, I'm just gonna lie here picturing you on top of me."

Jennifer winked.

Patrons from the restaurant started spilling out the front door cautiously surveying the burning wreckage. Jennifer had backed her air car into a slot between several other air cars. The van exploded just as it was making its turn to enter the lot. Two air cars partially shielded hers from the blast. The closest air car took the brunt of the damage. Less so for the next air car, and even less for Jennifer's. Her hood was pockmarked from flying debris and the windshield cracked on one side.

Just then Jennifer felt stinging in her right leg. She glanced down briefly at the few dots of blood her eyes registering the damage as minimal. She climbed atop the air bike and fired up the grav gen. The emergency wheels retracted and of course it worked fine—Leap Frog's breakdown was not real to begin with. Jennifer wheeled the air bike around tapping the break.

An air ambulance was moving fast coming from the direction of Sommerville down the road. Jennifer half expected it to stop to render aid, but realized that since its strobes weren't lit, it was going to rocket on by heading for the holding site. Jennifer smiled inwardly at her good fortune, twisted the throttle gently, then guided the air bike past the onlookers and off to the left pulling in behind her air-car. She hopped off, opened the back door, leaned in and grabbed what she needed. She shot her arm through the sling of the flechette rifle, draping the weapon against her back, then hopped back on the air bike. She twisted the throttle turning fast onto the road in pursuit.

Ochula watched Jennifer pick up speed following the air ambulance fighting the urge to jump behind the controls of the air car to help. Instead he padded over to the car weaving through the crowd, got in, then pulled out turning left heading in the opposite direction.

Jennifer got comfortable feeling the weight of the air bike between her legs and the strong wind pushing at her chest. The air bike was basically a naked sport bike with no windshield. She reached around her back grabbing the lump of her bum bag just to make sure it was still there, as was what was inside.

Jennifer wrenched the throttle pushing up her speed to stay with the ambulance. The journey to the holding site didn't take long. Jennifer had surveyed the geographic layout days earlier when she had done her initial recon at the restaurant/repair shop. The air ambulance up ahead was slowing at the guard shack checkpoint. The small shack fronted a ten-foot high dura chain-link fence topped with razor wire that surrounded at least two metal buildings of different sizes, some two hundred yards beyond. One building looked like it was maybe a-hundred-and- fifty feet to a side, and the smaller one off to the left, about twenty feet to a side. She accelerated hard to close the distance as fast as she could, then jammed on the brake coming to an abrupt halt just as the air ambulance stopped.

The man came out of the guard shack. He was momentarily distracted as he approached the driver-side window when he glanced back at Jennifer. She jumped off the air bike windmilling her arm in a looping arc. His eyes saw the choreographed move then looked up—catching sight of a small dark object floating through the air disappearing behind the back of the guard shack.

The fragmentation boomer detonated on the far side of the hut. Mangled metal was pushed out on a wave of concussive force and shattered glass launched at the speed of arrows spearing through the guard's torso without slowing. The man's pulped corpse bounced in a bloody splatter against the driver-side door of the air ambulance as the explosion pushed him away from ground zero. The boomer had turned the flimsy shed into a lethal antipersonnel bomb. The lifeless man poured into a puddle at the side of the van.

The driver reacted to the sudden detonation ducking in her seat for protection, then lifted her head cautiously spotting Jennifer for a brief instant in her side-view mirror. By the time her eyes registered Jennifer's presence, Jennifer jerked to a stop looking into the passenger-side window pointing the unslung flechette rifle at the two occupants. The flechette rifle spit wildly knifing through the open window raking the two fake medicos with lethal darts. Darts speared through ribs and heads, chewing flesh, bowling the passenger into the driver. Jennifer snapped out the partially spent magazine and rocked another one home as a wave of men rushed out of the smaller building two hundred yards beyond.

The men were in a panic amid the chaos not certain what was happening. Jennifer pressed her brief advantage, opened the door, pulled the dead passenger out, then lunged in yanking the driver through the door depositing the corpse on top of the other one.

She hopped in scrambling over the center console behind the controls. Terrified cries of panic registered in Jennifer's ears from the people in the back of the van. The victims would have to wait for an explanation. Jennifer stuck the rifle out the driver-side window pumping out rounds. The chattering flechette rifle ripped holes in the metal building forcing the group of hard cases to seek what little protection the ground provided. The men dug in covering their heads with their hands not able to return fire.

Jennifer knew she had pressed her advantage as far as it would go. She threw the rifle onto the passenger seat then grabbed the auto monocular from her bum bag. She flipped up the visor on the helmet and aimed the monocular at the cowering men anxious to extract any intel she could at such close range. She zoomed in quickly scanning the scared faces of the men as they began popping their heads up to look in her direction.

Jennifer's eyes exploded open with recognition. Framed in the sight was a man's face she recognized very well.

Shaking off her anger and confusion, she jerked the controls, jolting the air van hard around. She slammed the throttle rifling the air ambulance the way she'd come heading for the distant safety of the countryside.

Jennifer increased her speed to well over a hundred-and-ten miles per hour. Wind swirled in through both open windows of the air van. Because air cars rode on a cushion of generated gravity, the van didn't rumble and lurch. However, the dashboard vibrated and the high pitched whine of the straining grav gen was loud. Wafts of smell passed her face with the violently shifting wind in the cab. The gut wounds she'd inflicted on the two faux medicos had a foul smell that permeated the bloody mess painting the cab all around her.

The remaining blood mixed with the air and had a strong metallic twang to it.

The people in back were quiet now, realizing for the first time perhaps, that they were being taken away from danger instead of toward it—or they were just scared out of their minds. Jennifer concentrated on keeping the air van on the road trying not to think about the gory mess she was sitting in.

Several hard banked turns brought Jennifer closer to the rendezvous point with Ochula. *I have to ditch this vehicle fast,* she thought.

Constantly checking her six, Jennifer finally made it safely to the wooded forest of trees with the historical marker she'd visited a few days ago. Ochula was standing anxiously beside the rental air car when Jennifer screamed into the parking lot. She slammed to a stop, grabbed her weapon, then leapt out of the driver seat sliding the rifle sling hastily over a shoulder. Ochula followed her to the back doors pulling one side open while Jennifer yanked the other.

Inside were three people. A woman was gripping her two children to her chest trembling with the fear for the safety of her kids.

The tension in Jennifer's body retreated to insignificance locking eyes with the terrified woman.

"I won't hurt you. Please take my hand. Come with me."

The woman shot a jittery glance at Jennifer's outstretched hand. She gripped her two children harder finding it difficult to push aside a mother's instinct to protect.

Jennifer took a half step back, smiling sadly.

"Please, please come with me. We don't have much time to get your children to safety. Please," she pleaded not moving an inch closer.

The young woman hesitated then fought past her fear letting Ochula grab the small hand of her son. Jennifer reached in and lifted the three-year-old girl up onto her hip not backing away without the mother's look of approval. Finally the woman crab walked out the back of the van following Ochula and Jennifer to the air car. Ochula already had the doors open, but Jennifer didn't want to go around the other side of the air car with the small child. She was afraid that splitting up the two children, even placing the width of the air car between them, would surge a rise of renewed panic through the mother.

Both kids were silent as they clambered into the back seat followed by their mother.

Ochula shut the back door then climbed in behind the controls. Jennifer rounded the front of the car pushing the back door on her side closed before getting in the passenger seat.

Ochula guided the air car toward the air ambulance so that Jennifer could activate the incendiary boomer and toss it in back. He slowed enough for her to pitch it inside before accelerating the air car out of the lot turning right.

Everyone in the air car ducked down instinctively when the thundering boomer exploded behind them.

Ochula glanced over at Jennifer.

"You need to change," he said referring to her blood-stained clothes.

Jennifer was silent.

He tried again.

"Hey, you okay?"

She turned her head robotically, forehead deeply creased.

"No." Her voice strained to get the word out.

The air car picked up speed, Ochula banking it around a long corner heading further out into the countryside.

"You injured?"

When no reply came, he grabbed her arm shaking it.

"Jennifer, are you hit?"

The hurt in Jennifer's eyes seemed to escalate from a dull throb to a burning, glaring pain. It was a whole body reaction that had a life of its own.

"I found out who's behind it," she admitted. As soon as her hurt reached its peak, it was gone, receding into thin wind.

Jennifer turned in her seat gathering in the family she'd just saved. She seemed to extract redemption from their mere presence.

"I'm sorry I scared you."

The young mother searched Jennifer's harrowed face finding what she was looking for.

"I'm not." She pulled her five-year-old son tighter to her side with one arm. The other arm was wrapped around her daughter, holding her close. "I'm just glad they weren't armed like you."

"They should have armed themselves if they were going to abduct innocent children," Jennifer said roughly, the heat rising in her cheeks.

The young woman nodded imperceptibly, her eyes tense.

Jennifer looked at Ochula, calming herself.

"I do need to change," she acknowledged. "We're not going to head back to Sommerville until I know I'm not bringing trouble with us." She looked out the front windshield. "There's a quick mart I stopped at a few days ago about fifteen miles from here. It has a food counter with a few seats. While you take them inside I can change. My suitcase is in the boot."

Ochula nodded, feeling an icy breath on the back of his neck from Jennifer's admission earlier.

"Okay," was all he said.

Jennifer changed clothes in the back seat of the air car. Ochula had parked it on the periphery of the good-sized air car lot at the quick mart. Out in the countryside like this, space was not at a premium. The parking lot was paved closer to the store. Where Ochula parked was loose gravel with no real defined border.

Jennifer pulled in a long breath and exhaled resting a hand on the flechette rifle beside her. She had absolutely no intention of going into the quick mart while Ochula was in there with the family. Instead she scanned the scene around her with hyper-intensity. The adrenaline from the earlier fight was still coursing through her veins as was her rage about what she'd discovered.

No one is going to sneak up on me or this family, Jennifer promised herself silently.

Jennifer stepped out of the back seat standing close to the open door. She left the rifle in the air car for now.

Ochula held the hand of the boy as they walked behind the mother carrying her three-year-old towards the air car.

The four of them approached and Jennifer motioned with her head.

"Please get in on the other side."

Ochula guided the family around the back of the air car heading for the backseat door. Ochula opened it; the little girl jumped in followed by the mother and her son. At the same time Jennifer pulled the flechette rifle to her side holding it by the barrel and forestock down beside her leg shielding it from any potential onlookers in the quick mart. She shuffled back a few paces giving her enough room to close the back door.

Ochula came around the front of the air car stopping beside Jennifer. He held a stuffed plasti bag full of provisions.

Before Jennifer spoke her eyes did a full three-sixty survey of the surrounding countryside not spotting anything that set off her internal alarm.

Still shielding the rifle alongside her leg, she looked in Ochula's eyes.

"How are the kids?" Jennifer asked.

"Seem fine. I got them a milkshake. The mom ate something and the kids picked at a sandwich not finishing most of it." Ochula waited.

"The Prime Minister of Beltina was at the holding site, Ochula," Jennifer declared.

Ochula had seen a lot, been through a lot. He'd served in the Markem military coming up through the ranks starting as a grunt. Even when people were shooting back at him, he never lost his cool. Jennifer's statement was ominous—yes.

But given his background, not a total surprise. There was just one question.

"Why?"

Jennifer very carefully arranged her features so that she looked like nothing had happened at all.

"I don't know."

Ochula had half hoped Jennifer might know why Lad Blanconales was involved. He wasn't seeing the angle, the advantage of kidnapping innocent people. It just didn't make any sense. Ochula used a voice that gave comfort and no options in equal measure.

"I'm going to find out."

Jennifer liked the calm determination she heard in his voice. But first things first.

"We have to get away from here. We're exposed out here in the countryside."

Ochula didn't have to be told twice. He strode around the front of the air car getting in. Jennifer climbed in the passenger side as he powered up the grav gen then pulled quickly out of the lot.

Jennifer already had her head down looking at her hand comp screen.

"A couple options," she commented, her head still down. "Both keep us far away from Sommerville," she explained. "I want to put at least a full night between us and the firefight at the holding site before even thinking about going back to the spillway. "

Ochula had a good idea where she was headed with this. He'd already thought about the same options. He glanced in the rear-view mirror.

"Renata, you and your kids ever been camping before?" He asked them pleasantly, turning briefly to make eye contact with the mother.

Renata looked at each of her children in turn. Ochula had bought the boy a little spaceship toy. He was opening and closing the airlock hatch on it. Renata let him play with it then asked her daughter.

"GiGi, you want to sleep at a campground tonight?"

GiGi also had a toy. A doll with long hair. GiGi used the small brush that came with it to comb the doll's long locks. "Huh huh mm." She started talking quietly to the little doll, playing, not really paying much attention to her mom, just the doll.

Children had a tendency to be more resilient than grown ups. In this instance GiGi was more interested in her doll than being worried about being kidnapped again. On the other hand, Renata's son seemed more shaken, pulling his fear inwards.

Maybe it was more than that. Ochula just couldn't tell.

Jennifer knew that everything had to go through the mom before becoming a plan. She turned in her seat to find Renata looking into her eyes.

"I'm Jennifer by the way."

"Renata." She looked at her daughter and son in turn. "This is GiGi and AJ."

GiGi looked up at Jennifer.

"Hi, Jennifer. Did you see what Ochula got me?" She held up the doll still stroking the hair.

Jennifer gave a half smile.

"I did. Her hair looks nice."

GiGi pulled the doll back, murmuring to it, humming a tune as she combed its hair.

However, AJ didn't make eye contact. Jennifer sensed there was more to his reserved demeanor than being in the back of an air van when people were shot dead in front of him.

Renata seemed to pick up on Jennifer's thoughts but didn't try to explain.

"They've both been to city parks but have not spent the night at any of them. Ochula already mentioned something like that earlier." Her eyes tracked to the back of Ochula's head.

Ochula looked over at Jennifer.

"Yeah, we talked about that while we ate. She's okay with it," he confirmed speaking for Renata.

A thin smile lingered on Renata's lips looking at Ochula. She turned her head toward Jennifer.

"Whatever you think, Jennifer. I trust you," she confirmed.

Jennifer gave Ochula directions to a provincial park that took them over two hours to get to. On the way, Ochula stopped at a sports shop close to the camp ground to pick up a tent and sleeping bags for the family. Ochula and Jennifer would sleep in the air car. During that time she looked at the geography of the park on her HC. The park was located at the top of a foot-hill and had at least one alternate exit down the backside of the mountain where the campground was located. The entry gate was at the foot of the mountain and was self-serve.

Finally arriving at the park, Jennifer hopped out of the air car and went to the drop box where a map of the campsites was displayed. She tried to choose one on the front side of the mountain that would give her a view of the winding park entry road leading up to the campground. She selected site C-7 then touched her HC to the scan pad on the drop box to pay her creds for two nights.

The road wound its way up the mountain until it started to level off where campsites were numbered on a little sign next to each one. They passed two other occupied sites before coming to C-7 on the left up ahead. Ochula backed in killing the grav gen.

Renata got out with her kids and led them over to the lone picnic table.

Jennifer took the opportunity to pull Ochula aside. They stood behind the air car out of ear shot.

"You acted decisively just like you should have," she said referring to the drone strike.

"I had to wait for the black bag team to move on you before I zeroed them with the drone. I saw them coming hard down the road toward us but wasn't sure it was them until they yanked the hard right into the air car lot."

Jennifer smiled.

"You did good, really."

Ochula's brows dropped down focusing on Jennifer's injured right leg.

"You're hurt. Let me get you some wound wash and quick heal. I picked up what little first aid supplies they had in the quick mart."

Ochula started to turn to retrieve the plasti bag of provisions from the front seat, but Jennifer grabbed his forearm stopping him.

They locked eyes.

"I came here to find out who tried to kill me. It wasn't Lad Blanconales. At least I don't think it was. Why would he have asked Jeffrey for my help if he was just going to have me killed? I think he really does want to assimilate the IAs into Beltan society. What he's a part of with the abductions is completely unrelated to the assassination attempt on me. It has to be. There are two separate things at play here—the abductions and killing me."

Ochula considered what she'd said for a moment.

"We have to go somewhere safe, somewhere quiet to think through this. You know as well as I do that we have to set up a perimeter for tonight and stay vigilant. As a matter of fact, as soon as we clean your wounds, I intend to place motion activated vid cams on the park entry road. I want plenty of warning if someone comes up those switchbacks tonight. I can't think this through while I'm protecting this family, protecting us."

Jennifer agreed.

"I know. I'm just now dumping the adrenaline rush from earlier. I'm going to crash and burn soon as it is."

"You get some rest first then." Ochula glanced through the trees at the dwindling twilight. "It'll be dark in a few minutes. Nights are long on this planet. Grab some food then climb in the air car and crash. I'll set up the tent for the family then take first watch." Ochula watched Jennifer as he said all this, noticing the distracted look on her face. "What?" He asked.

Jennifer took in a breath pursing her lips.

"I said there are two things at play. I found out the prime minister is part of the abductions. What I really need to find out is who tried to kill me. I have a way to do that starting tomorrow at 11am."

Ochula twisted a side of this face.

"You're meeting with an informant tomorrow?"

"No, not an informant. Remember when you saw that terrified lady in the back of my air car yesterday morning? She's the arms dealer that sold the floater that nearly took me out. I conned her into telling me how she communicates with her client—the client that bought the floater. At 11am tomorrow I have a way to communicate with that client using the arms dealer's dead drop. I want to get a step closer to finding out who and why someone wants me dead."

"The why should be fairly easy, Jennifer. Don't you think?"

"Yes. I know what you're thinking. Someone wants me dead because they DON'T want me to help assimilate the IAs into Beltan society. That's secondary though."

Ochula wasn't following.

Jennifer continued.

"The who will tell us everything. Whoever it is, they have a lot to lose if the Insect Aliens become a part of Beltina." She blew out a breath. "Look, like you said we need to work on keeping ourselves alive tonight. We need to find a safe place to think this thing through. I just can't think straight enough now to sort it out."

"Let me get the first aid stuff, okay?" Ochula asked.

"Sure, thanks."

While Ochula was fetching the medico stuff, Jennifer opened the back door of the air car and sat down. She pulled off her trousers carefully and winced when the fabric scratched at her minor wounds.

Ochula bent down in front of her. Jennifer tilted the outside of her right leg so he could clean the dried blood spots with wound wash.

Jennifer grabbed his hand as he started applying gentle pressure to the first of four tender spots.

Ochula looked up into her grateful eyes.

Jennifer squeezed his hand harder.

"Thank you for saving my life."

ELEVEN

Ochula had picked up several self-heating coffee pouches when he'd stopped at the quick mart the day before. Jennifer was sitting on the top of the picnic table with her feet planted on the bench seat. She pulled the tab on a coffee and felt the outside of the pouch begin to warm heating up the coffee inside. While waiting for her coffee to heat, she watched the sun begin to come up over the backside of the foothill. She had taken the last watch of the evening over five hours ago. Ochula let her sleep much longer than she had intended.

Jennifer scooted off the picnic table making her way over to the air car. She took a pull on her beverage as the back seat of the air car came into view in the dim light of early morning.

To Jennifer's surprise Ochula and Renata were in the back seat alone. She had one leg draped over Ochula's leg and one hand pulling his face closer intimately. The two of them hadn't noticed Jennifer stop short sipping on her coffee.

Renata was about Jennifer's age, short and skinny, with a small waist and small breasts. Her jet black hair was pulled back in a ponytail. She wore brown trousers and a dark red short sleeved shirt.

Just then Jennifer thought of Krachy and how much she missed him.

Ochula was at least ten years older than Renata. He'd been single since Jennifer had first met him over four years ago. In all that time Jennifer had not seen or heard about him taking the time to be in a relationship. His lofty position as the head of Markem's military seemed to consume all his time and energy. Now that Ochula wasn't on Markem, wasn't doing his job, wasn't consumed as usual, he was letting out his feelings—joyfully by the look of it.

Jennifer turned fast not wanting to bother them or wake up the kids in the tent. There was some time before they had to get the day started to head back to Sommerville and the dead drop at the church.

About ten minutes later Renata and Ochula emerged from the back seat and strolled over to the picnic table Jennifer was sitting atop. The light was bright enough that Jennifer had seen the two of them untangle a few minutes earlier. She had taken the opportunity to pull the tabs on two coffee pouches so that they'd be hot when they got out of the air car. She had also devoured a pre-made sandwich and some corn crisps.

Jennifer smiled at Renata handing her a pouch.

Renata grabbed it.

"Thanks." She returned her look, took a few cautious sips, then leaned against Ochula wrapping her free arm around his waist. Ochula towered over her. He was nearly six-feet-four, Renata five-four or so.

Jennifer handed him the other pouch.

Ochula took it and used his other arm to pull Renata closer taking a drink. He looked at Jennifer.

"Get enough sleep?"

"Plenty, thanks."

Ochula's brows pulled together.

"You needed it." He glanced down at her injured leg. "Wounds need cleaning or are they healing?"

"I'm okay. The quick heal pulled the tiny pock marks closed overnight. I hardly feel anything now."

Renata pulled free from Ochula's grasp and stepped up onto the bench swiveling to sit down beside Jennifer on the table top. She set her pouch to one side then turned to look at Jennifer. Renata considered Jennifer's face, searching her eyes.

"I didn't thank you properly for what you did for us yesterday."

Jennifer never liked being the center of attention and would have done what she did for anyone in that same situation. She didn't know what to say. What she did know was now was not the time to let their guard down. They weren't clear of trouble yet. That realization washed over Jennifer's face hardening her features. Renata's gratitude seemed to heap that much more responsibility onto Jennifer's shoulders. Knowing that two children were her responsibility as well forced her to return Renata's gratitude with a guarded look.

"I would have done what I did for anyone caught up in that mess. Did Ochula tell you who I saw at the holding site? Who came out of the small building?"

"He did."

Jennifer's forehead rippled.

"And that doesn't worry you?"

"No."

Jennifer blinked.

"Ochula told me who you are."

"And you think that matters?" Jennifer asked skeptically.

Renata cocked her head, eyes moist.

"Yes. Not only can one person make a difference, they usually do."

Jennifer waited, clearly not liking the implication.

"Do you want to be that person?"

"No! I don't!" Jennifer thought back to all the people and beings she'd been forced to stop in the past. She hated that this was her mantra, her destiny. The same script replaying itself over and over like a sick play—a horrible phantasm of death and destruction.

"One step at a time, Jennifer."

Jennifer remembered what Darla said to her a few days ago—*act locally, think globally*. The thought sent an involuntary shiver through Jennifer.

Renata saw it.

"You're not responsible for my kids and I. You gave us a second chance. I intend to use it."

Ochula reached over tugging Jennifer's arm so she'd look at him.

"Hey. This is not all on you, Jennifer. I'm not going to let anything happen to this family."

When Jennifer didn't answer, Ochula's pupils dilated, eyes squinting.

"Nothing's going to happen to them while I'm around."

Jennifer flicked an uncomfortable look at Renata swallowing what she was about to say. Both she and Ochula were rested and could now think through what needed to be done next. But for an obvious reason Jennifer didn't want to involve Renata and her kids any more than necessary. Protecting, she was always protecting, continually siphoning off energy reserves in the process. It was scary how many times Jennifer had been pulled down into this pit of despair. She had come dirt-side alone to avoid this very thing—*No effin' luck!* Jennifer thought grimly.

Jennifer shook her head twice.

"I'm going to find out who has access to Laura Measures' dead drop. I can do that alone this morning. All I need is for you to take me there early so I can set up." Her eyes never left Ochula's on purpose.

Jennifer intended to take iron control of this situation and not get distracted heading down a labyrinth that didn't deliver value add. Lad Blanconales wanted to assimilate a new race into the population. Some groups would want this and others would not. But that was not Jennifer's problem. By avoiding this distraction she could keep the promise she had made to herself to find out who tried to kill her but injured Jeffrey instead. *I'm going to travel within this maze of deceit and confusion deftly,* she thought to herself. *I won't get sidetracked, and since I won't, Renata's family will never go anywhere near the clash between many competing forces. This is not my planet—not my responsibility.*

Ochula understood. He could see it in Jennifer's eyes. But he was also her friend.

"—At least let me watch your bac—" Before he could finish his sentence he got an alert ping on his HC connected to the remote vid cams he'd placed on the switchback road leading up to the park campground.

Ochula pulled his hand comp out of a pocket studying the screen. His forehead lined.

"A lone air car coming slowly up the hill. When it makes two more turns it will come into focus of the second vid cam. I can take a screenshot of the driver."

Less than twenty seconds later he snapped a pic with the push of a finger on the screen. He studied it but didn't recognize the man's face behind the controls of the air car. Ochula turned the screen toward Jennifer.

She looked at it, her eyes widening.

"That's Laura Measures' arms supplier."

"Who?" Ochula asked.

Jennifer pulled her eyes from the HC looking at Ochula.

"His name is GUNNY. He helped me extract the location of the dead drop from Measures yesterday morning. Remember the lady you saw that was terrified? Well, this guy is her supplier."

Ochula's lips pressed together into a threadlike stripe.

"I'm not going to let him get close to us whether you know him or not." His brows lifted.

Jennifer looked to one side as if considering what he said. The weight of reason pulled her gaze back to Ochula.

"I trusted this guy with my life yesterday, Ochula. I don't have time to explain but go easy."

"He's inside our perimeter. Remember what I told *you* yesterday," Ochula cautioned.

"He has to know I can defend myself. Hell, he provided the weapons. I'm not saying that you shouldn't be cautious, I'm just saying don't shoot a hole in him. Okay? He's coming in slow so we don't consider him a threat."

Renata interjected.

"He wants to talk," she deduced.

Jennifer looked side-long at her. "He wants to talk…I think so too. I'm going to speak with him."

Renata went back to the tent and climbed in with her kids who were still asleep. Jennifer and Ochula armed themselves keeping the boot lid open for easy access to more weapons if needed. They both slid a LP in their waistband and held a flechette rifle down by their side watching as GUNNY's air car made a slow approach to their campsite. The dense woods on either side and behind the campsite made a foreboding choke point hemming them in somewhat if things got out of hand.

Jennifer watched the air car stop in front of their campsite. Despite the perceived threat, Jennifer swiveled and decided to stow her flechette rifle in the boot. She knew Ochula had her back.

GUNNY stepped out of his air car arms at his side, hands empty.

Jennifer strode over to him stopping short.

"Hello, George."

George lifted an eyebrow only mildly fazed that she knew his real name.

"Hello, Jennifer."

Jennifer returned his look unshaken that he knew her name as well. Linden Kay had sent her a full run down on GUNNY right after she communicated with him the first time posing as Laura Measures. She had sent what information she had about him to her Security Officer and asked him to identify the man.

How George knew who Jennifer was wasn't all that unexpected. This man had a unique business that required unique skills to run. There was no doubt he had access to a reliable intelligence source of his own. He wouldn't be able to stay in business very long if he didn't.

Jennifer rubbed her lower back with a hand.

"My back still hurts."

"You wanted realism," George countered, shrugging an arm.

"I did," she agreed. "It's no coincidence you're here this morning is it?"

George didn't answer. Instead he studied her curiously with watchful, patient blue eyes. The arms dealer was about five-ten and looked to be in his late thirties with a wide mouth and dimples on each cheek. His light brown hair was full and parted to one side cut close but stylish. He seemed to take pride in his full head of hair and chose a cut that proved it. He was sturdy in the shoulders but thinning in the waist to the point of almost gaunt. Jennifer guessed that his pale features had more to do with a medical condition than not getting out in the sun very much. His skin was almost pasty, anemic in a way. George had on blue trousers, light blue shoes with white soles, and a slim fit full-zip black hoodie over a dark grey T-shirt.

"Where's the tracker?" Jennifer asked, slightly curious.

George shot a quick look over Jennifer's shoulder toward her rental air car then cast his duplicitous look at Jennifer.

"I stuck it up under the back bumper of your air car when Darla wasn't looking right before I closed in on you for the *kill*." The way he emphasized the word *kill* was playful. For the first time Jennifer sensed that he and Darla had quite a long discussion about how the faux stabbing would go down. She wondered why he trusted Darla so much—maybe there's more to it than that.

"You had me dead to rights. I'm very glad you're a man of your word. I trusted you and Darla and you both came through. Thank you."

"You're welcome. You're also right."

"What'da you mean I'm right?"

"About Darla."

"What about Darla?"

"No one has ever played me like she did the other night."

"What do you mean?"

"Darla had me dead to rights too. She could have blown my business up and let it crumble to the ground but she didn't. Two things—one, I admired what she did, the way she did it. And two—I admired what she didn't do. She didn't blow up my business and let it crumble. That would have been inconvenient, and not for the reasons you may think. Instead she gave me a lot more creds for very little work on my part. I looked her up last night and I told her what I thought of her. She's an awesome young lady."

Jennifer saw it now.

"You're sweet on her aren't you?"

"I'm trying to control that, Jennifer. She's young. I don't want to her to think badly of my intentions. We had a nice time last night that may turn into something more. I'm not going to flatter myself by saying it was just *my* idea to come and help you with the dead drop this morning. Darla insisted… very strongly…that I help you. To my meager credit, I've been toying over the idea seriously ever since Laura spilled it."

"And you had already placed the tracker on my air car…" It wasn't a question.

George's lips pulled tight.

"Habit." His forehead wrinkled. "I did a drive-by of the restaurant/repair shop on the outskirts of Sommerville before I went looking for Darla last night. You left quite a mess in your wake."

Jennifer put the pieces together. The tracker on her air car led him right to it.

"You don't know the half of it."

George looked away briefly as if the weight of the thing Jennifer had put in motion was unavoidable for him and his planet.

"I was afraid of that. The abductions are a pestilence poisoning my planet and everyone on it. They're pitting all of us against each other because we don't know who to trust. I believe that's exactly what the intent is, Jennifer."

This was an angle Jennifer had not considered. It worried her that she hadn't come to this conclusion herself. Her words came out in a breathy spurt.

"Blanconales is TRYING to forge fear and uncertainty?!"

"Has to be," George theorized. "Quite successfully too."

George Balliet is a smart man, Jennifer thought to herself. *I underestimated him. Glad that didn't bite me in the ass.* She let out a sigh of relief.

"I was never going to hurt you, Jennifer," George reassured as though reading her mind. "Just because Measures is a serious bitch and I scared the shit out of her doesn't mean I'd kill her either...I'm not like that. Besides, I have personal reasons not to do that. I checked on Laura last night when I visited with Darla."

Jennifer's face turned red realizing that she had tortured the woman, twice, and left her in a cage not bothering to check on her wellbeing more than she had. She felt ashamed and hated herself for her toxic temper—the means she always used to get what she wanted.

When Jennifer's head sagged, George took a step closer.

Jennifer saw his feet come into view of her downturned scowl then looked up into his eyes.

His look was complimentary.

"No one has taken it as far as you have. You just told me that Blanconales is behind the abductions. I didn't know that. I don't believe anyone did. I don't know why you've been given this burden, Jennifer. But don't stop. Don't ever stop."

"You never asked me why."

"I may know why. Not specifically—but partially. Someone wronged you or someone close to you. I know who you are to an extent. I even recognize the man standing over there near your air car. How could I *not* know him?"

Jennifer understood—or at least she thought she did.

"George, do you have a need to do this? To get involved. You keep hinting to personal reasons that are driving you. I think I had you pegged all wrong. Your motivation isn't greed at all, is it?"

"I have a lot to pay forward for what I've done, the things I've sold to others that have hurt and killed. Things are different for me now. Having my business shut down would have been inconvenient because it'd threaten my freedom. I'd be a fugitive. I can't afford that at this juncture. I need my freedom to do what I need to do. I made certain to provide the arms to who I thought was Laura the other night, but was really Darla, because I've long feared Laura would expose my operation and me too. That's the main reason I deal with that bitch, really."

George took a few steps back. He lifted the front of his shirt exposing what was underneath. Jennifer's eyes intensified staring at his stomach.

"I don't have that long, two maybe three months." His eyes cast down at the horrible cuts and scars crisscrossing his abdomen like a patch of tangled weeds. "Normally cancer like mine is easily curable if you catch it early enough. I didn't. I've always had a nervous stomach from the stress of my job. I just thought my gut was acting up more than usual. Then one morning I couldn't get out of bed. I had enough energy to call a friend so he'd take me to the hospital. There was no way I was gonna call for an air ambulance." He pulled his shirt down. "The operations I underwent took a lot out of me to delay the end two or three months, Jennifer.

"I want to do this for more than just me. Maybe for Darla, maybe for my planet. I don't really need much incentive at this point. If you were in my position maybe you'd understand. I've never had the chance to make a real difference. I've been selfish and done things, sold things I now regret selling. I don't have the time to debate it. I'm standing in front of someone that has made a difference in the past. Of that I'm sure. Plus getting a chance to work with a guy like Ochula Kozlov is not going to suck no matter how much the guy trusts me or not."

Jennifer's features softened, waiting. George was getting it all out—gushing on the person that made the most recent impact on his short life—her. It didn't matter who it was standing in front of him. He would be reaching for a purpose, a contribution, a summation to his life that meant something—he would be reaching for anyone at this point. Jennifer just happened to be at the wrong place at the right time in his journey.

Now I owe this man a legacy for him to leave behind. Can any one woman be forced to do things that she doesn't want to do more than me? I AM cursed...

"Darla is alive because of you."

The statement jerked Jennifer out of her crying game. She blinked.

George wouldn't let it go.

"I'll bet the family in that tent owe you something too." He took in a ragged breath and for the first time actually seemed like he was in pain—which he probably was. "I want in on that."

Jennifer clinched her jaw.

"Damn it! I keep telling everyone that I would have done what I did for anyone in that same situation. No one owes me anything!"

"And your point?"

"I don't have a point. I can't think straight now. You're heaping too much responsibility on me and I can't carry it. Okay, that's my point then...you get it!? Do you!?" She pulled out the vial of meds in her back pocket and dry swallowed two.

George watched her do it but didn't ask her about them. He didn't answer her either.

His silence seemed to chip away at her defiance. It was as though it had to be her and no one else. Finally, Jennifer had to ask even though she knew the answer.

"Did you see that mural under the spillway bridge at Darla's camp?"

George reached into his back pocket and pulled out his hand comp. He didn't even finger the screen before turning it toward Jennifer for her to see the picture already on the display.

"You mean this one?"

Jennifer squinted focusing on the screen. The bottom of her lips turned down crinkling her chin. Her breathing picked up pace, the in-out sound rushing out of her nostrils.

The mural had changed yet again. At the 8 o'clock position a streak of silver knifed down out of the sky until the bolt contacted the top of a white air van. The sides of the van were warped outward from the boiling orange explosion within. A concussion wave radiating outward in a uniform circular pattern depicted the blast wave quivering with explosive energy.

Jennifer looked at George angrily.

"There is no way they could have known what happened at the restaurant/repair shop, George! Darla, her friends, weren't even there!"

George dismissed her hostile glower with a chuckle.

"I saw what you did with one of my drones. I recognized the aftermath and walked in and talked to the old guy running the repair shop. He told me. He remembered you very well." His look turned impassioned. "Darla let me instruct her two friends that drew it. It's something I've never done before and I had the chance to do it with her. It was awesome."

The picture of the two of them, standing under the bridge, creating something together seemed like such a flippant thing to do considering the subject matter. But being in George's shoes made Jennifer rethink what she considered "inside the box thinking." At George's point in life he HAD NO BOX. The thought forced Jennifer to think about Darla and how much she liked her. And how much Darla had done for her without even asking. Jennifer asked something that she sensed earlier but was afraid to ask until now.

"How old are you, George?"

"Thirty-one," he replied like he knew exactly why she'd asked. His condition heaped at least seven or eight years onto his life clock.

Despite herself, Jennifer gulped.

George shook his head.

"I know how I look, Jennifer. It just means that I'm that much closer to Darla's age. A good thing, right?"

As Jennifer studied George, she felt her misguided anger skin away like an onion being peeled. With each rise and fall of his chest she knew he was one less breath closer to an abrupt end.

Jennifer's shoulders relaxed, her acrimony ebbing.

"C'mon then," she motioned with an arm. "Let's get you introduced to Ochula and Renata's family."

TWELVE

Jennifer looked over at George behind the controls of his air car.

After introducing him to Ochula and Renata's family, it made more sense for George to back her up when accessing the dead drop at the church on Abalong Street. George had been gushing out his feelings on Jennifer when they talked. But he didn't do that during the conversation with Ochula and Renata.

Jennifer knew Ochula's capabilities and ultimately would have preferred that he go with her to the dead drop. However, Renata's family was still a burden of responsibility that Jennifer and Ochula could not ignore. Plus, it was obvious Ochula liked Renata and her kids—a lot. And as much as she downright hated to admit it, if something bad happened to George she would feel less guilty. *Sometimes I'm an unfeeling mega-bitch,* Jennifer bemoaned to herself as she studied George. He had made a left turn and his head was canted away from her. She was glad that he could not see her eyes just then.

George came out of the banking turn staring straight ahead, no emotion on his face.

"I want to warn you of something, Jennifer." His eyes seemed to bulge from the sudden increase in blood pressure. George looked like he might be getting sick—but he wasn't. He was preparing to share something with Jennifer it seemed—something very important.

George didn't take his jittery eyes off the air car road. They were well within the city limits of Sommerville getting close to the dead drop.

Jennifer held back her questions.

What was this?

A few blocks from the dead drop George eased the air car behind a building in a deserted alley urging the air car to a slow halt. The way he gently brought the air car to a stop seemed like a lead into a foreboding premonition.

It was quiet in the air car when he powered down the grav gen. The only sounds were the two of them breathing.

George's breathing was harsh and irregular trying to control the weight of the threat he was picturing in his mind, his growing pain, or something else. He turned staring into her eyes.

"Some beings are worse than animals." His moist eyes gathered in the skull cap on Jennifer's head then landed on her narrowed eyes. "The brain coats the two of us are wearing won't protect us from the Insect Aliens dirt-side. The IAs may not be able to read our minds *right now* because of these anti-radiation silver-coated nylon caps, but that won't matter."

Jennifer was starting to rethink her earlier desire to have Ochula accompany her on this foray. George seemed to understand the threat they faced very well. Before she could ask he continued. He pushed on the controls to shift his body in his seat toward her for added emphasis.

"When you're an alien, you have to think on multiple levels and multiple dimensions." His head dipped. "You'd understand this if you thought like an Insect Alien."

Jennifer had the good sense to listen. It was obvious this man was going to teach her something she didn't know. Even with all the experience she had with the IAs, she realized that George knew things about them that she didn't. It was as though the tight lens Jennifer always used to assess the IAs was flawed. She had attached a constricting restraint that was preventing her from seeing the big picture. That restraint was obvious to her now—it was her fierce temperament.

George's eyes narrowed and he squinted.

"Look, you may have swallowed the revenge-is-a-good-thing fable, Jennifer, but I haven't. I don't believe that all you care about is killing the beings responsible for hurting someone close to you. Get vengeance on a few Insects Aliens that pissed you off? No way. Feel satisfied after you kill the ones responsible? Implausible. Leave Beltina afterwards and live happily ever after? Inconceivable."

Jennifer took a long look around outside the air car, her mind concluding the futility of it all.

"We shouldn't even go through with this, should we, George?"

"I really do not think the people that care about you will be happy when you end up dead later this morning."

George seemed to prompt a sensibility in Jennifer that she didn't even know she possessed until now.

"Habit," Jennifer admitted.

"I understand your drive and I respect it. But I assure you it's misplaced."

"We're overmatched, aren't we, George? You knew that before we got in the air car to head this way, didn't you?"

"I figured if I had some alone time with you I could get you to understand that. I wasn't completely sure. One look at that mural, and talking with Darla last night, convinced me you had it in you."

"That mural is the bane of my existence."

George shook his head.

"The IAs had you figured out even before you came dirtside. You were never going to get revenge on the few of them that hurt whoever it was that's close to you. What I said before goes doubly true for your misguided mission. These aliens think on multiple levels and in multiple dimensions. While you're a smart lady, you aren't all that hard to figure out. If I can do it in a few hours what does that tell you?"

The bottomless pit holding her anger was the bane of her existence—not a silly mural. Then something occurred to Jennifer.

"You know about the splinter faction of the Insect Alien Collective, don't you, George?"

"That group has been monitoring everything you've been plotting since you started. There was no way you were going to outsmart them. The real play is right out in the open for everyone to see."

"They don't want the IA Collective to be integrated into the Beltan society because they want to remain the rogue group that they are. They want to remain independent. Right?"

"Of course. And they've succeeded in stopping you from helping Blanconales. With what you now know about what he's done, you would never help him now. They played you and you didn't even know it, Jennifer."

"But the rogue IAs don't control Blanconales."

"No they don't. Blanconales chose to do what he's doing for his own selfish reasons. What you and Ochula have not asked yourself this whole time is the RIGHT question."

Jennifer's brow scrunched.

"You and Ochula have been asking the wrong question. The question is not *WHY* is Lad Blanconales abducting and holding innocent people. The right question is *WHEN*? Think about what's happening soon—planet-wide elections for prime minister.

"The PM is trying to keep power by forging fear and uncertainty. Blanconales has effectively plunged Beltina into distrust in a bid to take advantage of that atmosphere to improve his chances of winning the upcoming election. What I'm talking about is not an unreasonable assumption. Fear works! Fear gets votes, gets backing. Leadership is followed. Blanconales has not unveiled his plan to assimilate the IA Collective into Beltan society. But he will. He will very soon. Then he'll use that announcement to stop the abductions claiming the IAs used their telepathy to help him. Then he'll be able to assimilate the IAs with success and without opposition. Any opposition will crumble."

Jennifer tilted her head quizzically.

"Then why did he want me to be the IA Ambassador?"

George grunted.

"So the rogue IAs would kill you. Blanconales knew this and he tried to pull you into a trap. If you and I would have tried to access that dead drop this morning he would have succeeded. The rogue IAs would have killed you."

George powered up the grav gen. It hummed to life lifting the air car up. He pushed at the controls, urging up the speed, turning right at the end of the building to get as far away from the dead drop as possible. He started weaving his way quickly out of town.

Jennifer looked out the front windshield scanning the road ahead. She outstretched her right hand placing it on the dash; the other hand gripped the back of George's seat so that she could pivot her head out the back to look for trouble.

"They may still succeed." Her head turned checking their six then the street ahead in a slow back-and-forth motion trying to spot danger before it happened. Her anger ticked up another notch.

"I made a mistake pulling us into downtown Sommerville. Until we get into the suburbs, these tight streets are hemming us in if things go south. I apologize."

George Balliet frowned at Jennifer. His anxious expression had frosted into something impatient and mean.

"This foray puts me in jeopardy. It puts us both in jeopardy. You haven't been wearing a brain coat the entire time you've been dirt-side have you?"

"No." Jennifer wanted to ask, *If you knew the answer, then why did you bring it up?* But unfortunately, she already knew the answer.

"You didn't think of it. It makes me wonder what else you're missing," he scolded.

Jennifer glanced over at him and asked, "You want to tell me what's really bugging you?"

"This whole situation. Specifically, your selfish approach to it."

George didn't pull his punches. Jennifer thought back to what he said when they first spoke earlier that morning. *I don't have time to debate it.*

"Think of the exposure you unduly placed us both in, Jennifer."

Then Jennifer thought she understood. It wasn't about George's safety. It wasn't about her safety either. It was about his chance to make a difference. Her selfish need for vengeance could deny him of that and he was pissed off—royally pissed off!

His lips started to thin out of anger. He shook his head and muttered something to himself. Jennifer was glad she couldn't understand what. Her cheeks heated but not in anger—in embarrassment. George went back to driving and an instant later she saw him raise an arm, too late to do anything about it. He hit her on the top of her skinny thigh with a thunderous hammer fist.

Jennifer yelled out. "Shit!"

"Don't you make light of me," he warned. "I am not happy about this."

"Damn it!" Jennifer yelped. "I was trying to admit I screwed up."

"Yeah, well, find another way."

They drove in silence for a few minutes finally heading out into the suburbs. Jennifer rubbed her thigh thinking that she was probably going to have to ice it when she had the chance. George knew what he was doing and had really nailed her.

Seeing how pissed off and resentful he was forced Jennifer to feverishly search for another way to approach this situation. She did swallow the revenge-is-a-good-thing fable. But it wasn't a fable—it had been bait that was dangled out in front of her. Bait to lure her into a trap. And she had to admit to herself, on even the most basic level, that killing the beings responsible for hurting Jeffrey was not the only thing she cared about. Since first seeing the abductions, she wanted to stop them. She had even acted on that—saving Darla, saving the homeless people at the air ambulance wreck, saving Renata's family, and yes, even saving Laura Measures.

Jennifer decided that taking several of Blanconales' abduction teams off the board was a start.

Jennifer felt her hand comp vibrate in her pocket, glad for the distraction to cut the tension in the air car. She accepted the comm and pulled it to her ear.

"Hey." It was Ochula.

"Hey."

"I got the family safe," he said, careful not to mention any names or places. "I've spent the last hour gathering some intel. We need to talk, but not on an open channel. Meet me at the place before our long drive yesterday."

Jennifer understood where that was. It was the quick mart out in the country.

"We'll be there shortly." She cut the comm.

George seemed to be brooding as he guided the air car further out into the countryside. Jennifer fingered the screen on her HC then turned it toward him so he could see it.

"Can you take us here?"

He glanced at the location and nodded once. His silence was like a wall of distrust.

Jennifer decided that she had to begin cutting through it or they wouldn't be able to make any progress.

"Look, you've put me in my place and thumped me hard. We can work together as a team. I can do that, can you?"

There was a pause. George answered, "Yes I can."

Even as cranky as George was, and all the flaws that he'd pointed out in her, Jennifer wanted to help him. She knew that helping him would help others. On the one hand, she didn't want him to think she was a liability which she knew she wasn't—usually. On the other hand, she was smart as he'd pointed out. On the other hand…

Jesus. I can't take much more of this.

"Stop!" He barked, sensing her doubt. "You understand now. We can find another way. With Ochula helping, I'm sure of it." He banked the air car right looking at her, "Aren't you?"

Jennifer nodded quietly.

THIRTEEN

The drive to the quick mart was thankfully uneventful. Ochula had parked Jennifer's air car rental on the back side of the mart in an effort to give he, George, and Jennifer an alternate egress should trouble arise. George's air car was parked out front. The three of them scrunched into a booth in the corner of the little cafe section of the quick mart. There were three booths plus a counter with six barstools. Windows lined the periphery of the cafe nook which allowed them to look out into the countryside in several directions.

Jennifer waited for George to start talking while she cracked the tab on a self-cooling ice pack. She'd bought it when they arrived. It was resting on her sore thigh now.

Ochula looked side-long at her but didn't say anything. He too seemed to be waiting for George to start talking. The time was just past 11am. Ochula knew their arrival time meant that Jennifer did not go through with her plan to access the dead drop. This didn't seem to phase him. He didn't ask her why she'd bailed out.

Jennifer was glad she didn't have to explain herself. She had a headache that was growing in magnitude.

George turned his head from looking out the window fixing his gaze on Ochula and Jennifer seated across from him. The three of them sipped on a thermo tumbler milkshake each.

"I let Jennifer know that pursuing the dead drop was a bad idea," he explained. "She took some convincing," he remarked referring to her leg.

Ochula was unruffled but looked at Jennifer just to make sure.

"So you're okay with that, Jennifer?"

"Yeah." She repositioned the ice pack shooting a hard look at George before returning her eyes to Ochula. "He was right. That would have been a mistake. George has a solid idea why Blanconales is abducting peopl—"

"—The upcoming elections," Ochula interjected.

Jennifer wasn't surprised he knew. This had to be part of the intel he mentioned earlier during their comm.

"Yes," she confirmed.

"Well, I spoke with Ian. I felt I had to contact him to let him know that I was dirt-side. It was a courtesy comm that turned into something more."

Jennifer's face warmed not liking being reminded that she didn't tell Ian about Ochula's help before now. *What else am I missing?* She took a moment to pop two pills into her mouth washing them down with a few frigid swigs of vanilla shake. Her hand shot to her forehead and rubbed at her temples like she was upset with herself, getting sick, was getting brain freeze, or a combination of all these things.

Ochula placed a hand on her forearm pursuing the most logical reason.

"You're pushing hard, Jennifer."

Her hand came down and she looked at his hand on her arm for a brief instant. Jennifer scanned his face.

"I know. What else am I supposed to do?"

"Let us help you." He removed his hand. Ochula looked over at George then back into her eyes. A faint smile edged his lips.

"It's just your nature. You can't help it sometimes. I'm glad you didn't have to chin somebody at the dead drop to get the info you wanted. They may have chinned you instead."

"You're not mad at me?"

When Ochula's look glazed over, Jennifer cleared her throat.

"Was Ian mad at me?"

"He didn't seem to be, no. What? You think I'm upset? Well, I'm not. Not at you anyway. I want to stop Blanconales. Ian had me speak with Linden." Ochula turned to George. "George, Linden is Jennifer's Chief Security Officer. He told me what he found out."

"And?" George lifted a brow.

"A couple of things." Ochula took several swigs of his shake. "He believes that Blanconales was at the holding site near Sommerville to check on things, not much more. It was a coincidence that Jennifer rescued Renata and her kids at the same time Blanconales was there. Besides, Jennifer had on an air bike helmet at the time. He can't know with absolute certainty it was her that attacked. Although, he does know what she's capable of. Either way, he'll probably move on to another holding site tomorrow, making his rounds so to speak. This mess is planet-wide."

"How does any of that help us help Jennifer?" George asked.

"Two things—one, we may have a window to catch the holding site near Sommerville off guard. And two—Blanconales has a weakness we can exploit if we choose to do so."

Jennifer pulled her drink from her lips as she was about to take another sip. Her eyes rounded.

"Are you talking assassination?"

"Yes." Ochula answered flatly.

George blew out a soft whistle.

"You don't mess around do you, Ochula? I only had the holding site piece figured out."

"Wait a minute!" Jennifer's voice rose unconsciously. She dialed back her adrenaline a bit. "Slow down! Explain to me exactly what you mean by a window at the holding site. Start with that."

George answered for him.

"The holding site is supposed to be a covert operation, drawing little or no attention, and in the past few days since you've arrived, the immediate area in and around it, and Sommerville, has exploded in to several major gunfights. Violence against Blanconcales' plans isn't common. The faux first responders have been carrying out their abductions with impunity. To have so many of their ranks end up dead in the space of a few days would put them on alert."

Jennifer wasn't seeing the angle. Her condition slowing her…

When Jennifer didn't respond, George eyed her. He pulled his drink down after swallowing a gulp. His eyes narrowed threateningly, revealing the look of a calculating predator.

Then Jennifer saw it.

"If the Sommerville holding site is on alert, then the hostages will either have to be moved or worse…" Her breath caught. "Or killed—"

Ochula broke in, sensing the urgency of time.

"—How good are those pills you took?"

Jennifer tensed, her heart rate rising.

"You mean now?! Hit the holding site now?!"

"Later. We wait for darkness."

"If somehow we manage to take out the facility and rescue the hostages, there's still one dangling thread."

"I know—Blanconales. I told you he had a weakness. He'll be exercising that weakness this evening. Linden has what I consider solid intel. He's crafty and looked deeper into Blanconales' background. He also told me about his idea for a *twofer*. Well, nighttime on Beltina is long. We hit the holding site then we hit Blanconales—a twofer. He'd never expect that. Not to mention where he'll be when we hit him gives us an advantage. He may not even be taking comms while he's partaking in his weakness." Ochula's sneer was devious.

Jennifer had to ask.

"You aren't afraid of the intergalactic scandal this will cause if your participation in all this is uncovered? This could lead to war with Markem again, Ochula. You have to know that. You have to!"

"What I know is the penalty for inaction, Jennifer. I can't live with myself if Blanconales picks the second option."

"The second option?"

"Can you live with yourself if Blanconales decides the hostages aren't worth keeping? If he kills them? I wouldn't put anything past him at this point. You shouldn't either."

George cracked a smile.

Jennifer noticed.

"You're eating this up aren't you, George?" She shook her head at this man's gall—even though she totally understood it.

"I told you it wouldn't suck working with Ochula no matter how much he trusted me or not." He paused, then, "Act locally, think globally."

Jennifer certainly knew where that advice came from.

***

When Jennifer stopped short in front of the dura chain-link fence door to Laura Measures' improvised detention cell, Measures pulled her eyes up from the small plasti tray of food she was working on. Her eyebrows rippled nervously spotting her tormentor. The right eye swelling had receded a good bit but still looked tender.

Jennifer held her hand comp in one hand while she fished in a pocket digging out the padlock key then used it to click open the lock. She pulled the door open and took a few steps back.

"You can go, Laura," Jennifer asserted.

Measures' eyes tensed, her eyeballs darting side-to-side trying to determine if this was another trap or not.

Laura was right to be skeptical. It WAS a trap. The threat was written all over Jennifer's face.

She finished chewing and swallowed cautiously setting the tray down beside her but didn't stand up. No way Jennifer didn't have a weapon on her.

Finally Measures ventured a soft breath.

"That's it, no catch?"

"Not exactly." When Jennifer pulled her HC to her face fingering the screen, Measures' body jerked back at the movement clearly expecting something deadly to be pointed at her instead.

Jennifer finished touching the screen then let the hand comp fall gripped in her hand.

Measures frowned.

"I don't want you to burn my other eye."

"I don't want to burn your other eye either."

Measures' frown deepened.

"What then? What do you want before I can get as far away from you as possible?"

"Help." Jennifer's lips turned up slightly. "If you don't help, I won't hurt you again. Not you anyway..." She let that hang in the air ominously.

The HC display was turned toward Measures enough that she could identify the pic on the screen. Since Measures was on the ground, it was about eye level.

The hair on the back of Laura Measures' neck bristled, her eyes snapping open aghast to what was on the screen. Measures could not take her eyes off the pic. A few tears welled up in her eyes then dribbled down both cheeks.

Jennifer's voice was calm.

"I said I won't hurt you again if you don't help. I mean that." She shot a baleful look at the HC pic Laura was fixated on.

Measures' jaw clinched and she felt like exploding to her feet and wrapping her hands around the scrawny neck of the bitch that'd threaten such a thing. Jennifer saw her body tense and quiver with hate.

"You do this one thing for me and we're even. I'll give you back your HC and you can get back to business. You can even continue to enjoy *her* company while doing it. It's a generous offer, Laura—very," Jennifer maintained.

Measures wiped at her cheeks with a sleeve sniffing. The hate behind her eyes seemed to recede into resignation. She had no choice. She knew that and was certain Jennifer intended the threat to mean exactly that. The pic confirmed it all.

Measures sniffed again gaining back some composure.

"I don't want you to hurt Jenny!" Laura Measures was a tough woman, healthy and strong, and more specifically, a lesbian. Jenny was her partner—her one and only. Laura loved her like no other. The HC had Jenny's pic on the screen.

"You go back to your flat and get cleaned up. GUNNY will take you there and wait while you make yourself presentable. He'll explain on the way."

When Laura's eyes narrowed at George's name, Jennifer remarked, "And no, George is not going to set you up again. That was all my idea anyway. After you're done, he's going to take you to a place in Sommerville to reconnoiter. Familiarize yourself with the place, the area. You'll know what to do by then."

Resigned, Laura stood up slowly. Her impulse to club Jennifer in the side of the head was overwhelming but she resisted. The fight to do nothing was written all over her face.

"Laura, I know you hate me right now for threatening to hurt Jenny. How do you think I feel about you after what you did? George convinced me earlier today that my own hate was misplaced just like yours is now. Maybe when we meet up again later this evening, after spending some time with him, you'll understand. I hope so."

The tone of Jennifer's voice allowed Laura for the first time, within accepted bounds, to actually see Jennifer as a person, not a predator.

"What are you saying?"

"I'm saying you're going to want to help me. And not because of Jenny." Jennifer fingered the side button snapping her HC off, Jenny's pic disappearing. "Maybe while you're with George you'll realize I actually saved your life—twice. I didn't blow a hole in your head at your flat and I pulled you out of the air ambulance and brought you here."

Laura was unconvinced.

"You tortured me THEN set me up to be abducted by that air ambulance."

"And I corrected both of those actions, Laura. You haven't forgotten what type of business you're in have you? You should see what condition the man that saved my life from that exploding floater you sold is in! If not for him, I wouldn't even be standing here trying to pound some sense of responsibility into that hard head of yours." Jennifer's chest rose and fell. "Jeffrey means a lot to me! You're not without blame here!"

When Laura didn't respond, Jennifer controlled her rising anger mindful of time pressures.

"As hard as it is for you to believe now, you're going to trust me before the night is out."

Jennifer lifted her arms and did a slow circle showing Laura that she did not, in fact, have a weapon stashed away anywhere on her.

"Believe it or not, I already trust you."

Jennifer knew the risk she was taking was very real. She also knew that she had enough leverage to be relatively certain Measures would acquiesce without violence. But as George had made all too clear—she didn't have the time to debate it.

"George is waiting atop the spillway."

Laura's eyes seemed to accept her fate—her non action tacit proof of that. She stepped out of the cell, brushed past Jennifer, and hiked up over the crest of the spillway out of sight.

FOURTEEN

Jennifer heard the knock on the pocket door of the hotel room then pushed the back of her hand to the scan pad. The door moved aside. George was standing in the hallway with Laura Measures a few paces behind him looking sullen. The sullen look was only on her face; her body looked stunning, as what she was wearing. Or more appropriately, what she was not wearing. Jennifer couldn't help but notice.

Jennifer and Ochula had decided to get a hotel suite where this meeting could take place privately. Besides, Jennifer had no intention of exposing Darla and her friends any more than necessary.

"Come in," she turned and led them both into the two-bedroom suite. The large living area was arranged with a L sectional low couch in the front of a table and chairs and a big floor-to-ceiling window with the drapes pulled shut. A rectangular coffee table was in front of the sectional with what looked like a small engineering blueprint on top. The time was just past 6pm.

Laura shuffled nervously into the room stopping just past the short entry hall. Her arms folded awkwardly over her accordion-like bare stomach protecting it from Jennifer's undue attention. She liked Jenny looking at her but not this Devil Bitch From Hell. Her head sagged but she lifted her eyes when Jennifer approached her.

Laura was wearing a white hollowed out drawstring waist form-fitting short skirt and a white and orange striped one-shoulder sleeveless knit top that was almost a bralette—it barely covered the underside of her breasts. The color choice amplified her stout nipples and dark tanned muscular skin underneath, as did the white closed-toe high heel ankle-strap stilettos on her feet. The sharp angle of the heels flexed her bulging, ripped thigh and calf muscles all the more. With less than six percent body fat from years of training, Laura's choice of an incredibly simple yet striking outfit showed that she knew what she was doing to show off all the work she had done. Her outfit was complemented by a heart pendant choker that hid her injured throat and oval-shaped metal sunglasses that concealed her damaged eye. Her dark brown hair was smooth against her scalp pulled back into a ponytail accentuating her high cheek bones.

Jennifer didn't waist any time—she had no choice either.

"It's time for you to get into character, Laura." With that statement Jennifer reached out and pulled Laura's hands away from her stomach. She let go, but Laura curled her arms around her belly slowly.

Laura did not like this woman staring at her.

Jennifer's eyes ignited.

"Stop that, Laura!" She growled. "You're not going to be any good to us, or your planet, if you look like a sixteen-year-old teeny going out on a first date. You need to be alluring and confident. Hell, I know you have that persona in you. George commed me and told me you got the job at *Rumors*. Just get with the program. This is all gonna be over by tomorrow morning." Jennifer shot her hands to her hips retreating several steps.

The room was noticeably quiet for a moment.

Laura's arms dropped to her side, the sinuous lines of her cut arms flexing. Her eyes became slits fixing Jennifer with a glower.

"I'll do my part, but why should I believe you'll leave Jenny be when this is over?"

"If you don't trust me right now that's fine. I only said you'd trust me when the night is over. Maybe you'll trust this guy."

Laura's brow pinched.

"What guy? George?"

"No," Jennifer corrected, then jerked a thumb over her shoulder at the tall man that had just entered the room from one of the bedrooms.

Laura's eyes fixed on the familiar face of Ochula Kozlov through the optics of her sunglasses. She reached up and pulled off the shades slowly, her brown eyes staring openly, mouth ajar.

Jennifer's voice cut into her stupor.

"Well?! What's it gonna be?"

Laura was at a loss for words. Her mouth went slack.

Ochula strode over to her, all the while Laura's eyes growing in size, until Ochula stopped in front of her reaching up to push her gaping mouth shut with an audible *hap*.

Laura stammered.

"—I, you're—"

Ochula took a half-step back reaching down grabbing the sunglasses with both hands then gently placing them back in place on her face.

"I'm who you think I am, Laura. Jennifer has been my friend for a long time. Your planet and mine were at war once. Jennifer helped broker the ceasefire. I couldn't have done it without her. And tonight, I can't stop your prime minister from hurting countless more victims without you. Whaddaya say to that?"

Laura's chest pulled in a breath like she invariably did when the weight on the barbell she was about to lift was going to submit to her strength. This was how she always overcame indecision—determination and nothing but determination, clinching her entire body rigid in defiance.

"I say that Jennifer has powerful friends, and I think I believe you."

"Well, that's a start at least. Come sit down so we can study the layout of the pleasure club Blanconales is going to be at this evening. I printed out an old-fashioned drawing so you can walk us through it. You're the only one that's actually been inside."

Laura seemed to transform as she watched Ochula take a seat on the low couch then turned to Jennifer. Her voice rose in pitch.

"I had no idea you knew Commander Kozlov." She turned to George. "You didn't mention the head of Markem's military was involved in this."

Her muscles released along with the hate-filled tension she had bottled up in them. Laura knew she was a specimen having looked at, flexed, sculpted, strained, and enhanced every part of her body to achieve the required look of a competitive body-builder. She had posed alongside some of the most impressive female athletes on the planet, but had never won the championship, having placed third three times. Still, when she strutted over to the couch, it was obvious Laura remembered what it was like to have the eyes of thousands of adoring fans scrutinizing every inch of her perfect body.

Ochula could almost hear Laura's rock-hard inner thighs brush against each other like sand paper when she crossed the living room. Even he couldn't pull his stare off her—both eyes trying to determine which luscious part of her fit body he liked best. He shook himself from his reverie inwardly admitting that ALL of it looked delicious.

When she plopped down on the low couch next to him, her firm boobs didn't even bounce with the impact.

She locked in on his eyes looking at them.

"You can cup a nice handful if you don't think they're real," Laura offered breezily. "About two percent of the fat in my body are in them—the rest is in my rock-solid ass." An eyelid arched along with the same corner of her mouth.

Ochula's face didn't redden and he didn't pull his eyes from her chest for a full ten seconds. Then he looked into her eyes, the corners of his mouth rising playfully.

"I can see why *Rumors* is letting you start tonight." Laura exaggerated shifting sideways on her left ass cheek so that Ochula could get a smell of her womanhood, then raised her right leg draping it over the other leg slowly crossing them. Her tight skirt lifted toward her crotch trying to fight the size of her hardened thigh but lost the battle. She flexed her quadricep, and her skirt slid down further revealing that she had no panties on, not even a thong, hiding any of her yummy girl goods.

Laura casually glanced down at her shaved she-area then back into Ochula's eyes.

"The Fixer that interviewed me at *Rumors* was a right perv. I flashed him just like I'm flashing you. He hired me on the spot." The way she said "right perv" made it clear she had significant distaste for men in general *and* their predictable urges.

Ochula couldn't help but comment. He seemed fine to play along even though he knew it could never, ever, lead anywhere.

"You're good at that. I mean doing what you're doing to me. Seems really natural," he declared, referring to her expert ability even though a lesbian. Not surprisingly, Ochula felt his pants tighten.

"Men were always the judges at the competitions I entered. If I didn't know how to differentiate my product, I would have never come as close as I did to winning all those times."

Jennifer watched the by-play between the two of them patiently. *Laura was going to do just fine.* All she had to do was be inside the pleasure club at the right time this evening. Ochula, George and her would do the rest—she hoped.

Despite being willfully aroused, Ochula needed Laura to get down to business.

"Can you please turn that off now? It is distracting."

With that Laura uncrossed her legs pulling her short skirt down toward her knees. She scooted herself away from Ochula then clasped her hands together over her kneecaps looking thoughtfully at the diagram on the coffee table.

"Thank you," he said.

Laura's provocative fragrance lingered next to him where she had just vacated the space. His nose gathered in her amorous scent with three words coming to mind to name it— *Seductive Bed Sheets*.

Ochula felt the weight of Jennifer's stare on his face and looked up at her.

She crinkled her mouth, dimpling her chin.

"Confidence taken in, by a sun tan and a grin." She shook her head crossing her arms.

Jennifer had him nailed cold, but he decided to deflect the blame anyway.

"She initiated it—"

Jennifer interjected.

"—Still initiated..." Her eyes drifted down to his pitched tent.

Laura's eyes remained fixed on the diagram. Pitched tents didn't interest her. She pointed.

"The entry lobby is wrong. But the rest of the drawing looks pretty accurate. What are the grid lines for?"

Ochula had taken the public records file Linden had obtained from the Provincial Registrar of Deeds Office in Sommerville, printed a copy, then drawn grids on the building layout. Across the top, columns were labeled A, B, C...etcetera. Down the left side numbers denoted each row starting with "1" at the top.

Ochula figured it would make it easier for all of them to pinpoint room locations or any other feature they wanted to focus on, for example A 4—the entry lobby.

Jennifer uncrossed her arms but didn't move to look over Laura's shoulder. She didn't want to be out of her line of sight or add any tension to what she already knew was hovering in the air between them. Instead, she stepped over to the far side of the coffee table across from Ochula to study the diagram upside-down.

George, silent this whole time, seemed in complete control of his own primal urges despite Laura's performance. He had to admit that it did take some doing to ignore her provocative exhibition. But that was made easier by repeating to himself, *Laura's still a bitch, Laura's still a bitch...*over and over. He sat down perpendicular to Ochula and Laura on the low couch surveying the blueprint.

"A 4 is the lobby you're talking about, Laura," Ochula explained. "The grid helps us zero in on a place in the club more quickly. You see?"

"Yeah," Laura nodded. She turned to Ochula.

"Before we go over what's inside the club and what you need me to do, I just wanted to hear from you that you actually intend to kill the prime minister tonight. The plan George explained will limit my exposure but I could very easily get pinched, or worse, if this thing blows up."

"Did George tell you why we think it's necessary to take Blanconales out?"

"Look, Ochula, I'm not stupid!" Laura snapped. "I've seen what's been happening on my planet. George told me Blanconales is responsible and I believe that too." She flicked an irritated look at Jennifer briefly. "I was almost a victim of one of the abductions if not for her getting religion or something to pull me out of it. But this is a massive ask of me. Even with you holding my feelings for Jenny over me, I may end up dead if you three screw up."

George listened silently hearing the clip in her tone. The real Laura had to surface eventually. It was boiling near the surface for sure. He waited to see how Ochula would handle it. He was certain Ochula could; he was just curious to see how he did. Through all of this, George was, if nothing else, enjoying the show.

This is just the type of action I needed before I go out, he thought to himself.

Jennifer spotted the imperceptible smile on George's lips, leaned down, and pulled at his bicep, her eyes thinning into razor slits.

"George, did you tell Laura about your condition? She has a right to know."

Jennifer let go and stood staring down at him. She didn't like that he couldn't control his excitement about how all this was playing out. While she understood it, she wanted Laura to have the chance to understand it too.

Laura WAS risking a lot to help them *and* her planet. Jennifer also didn't like holding a young woman that she'd never even met over Laura to force her to help. The air needed to be cleared before this mission went any further.

When George hesitated, Laura asked, "What condition?"

Jennifer was silent, waiting.

George cleared his throat.

"I'm dying, Laura—cancer."

While Laura didn't particularly care for George as a human being, the statement was ominous. Laura caught herself glancing up at Jennifer for confirmation.

Jennifer's lips tightened and she dipped her head once.

This was the first crack in Laura's armor. Something she absolutely did not expect so soon in the evening. *Siding with Jennifer on anything was an impossibility, wasn't it?*

Jennifer saw the revelation form behind Laura's eyes but said nothing.

Laura returned her look to George studying him. She had assumed his outwardly diminished physical condition over the last few months was self inflicted. Maybe hitting on too many vape sticks, living hard enjoying the many perks of being a successful arms dealer, or partaking in the euphoric drug Gleam too much. But that wasn't the case at all. It made her feel somewhat ashamed that she hadn't asked before now. Despite herself, she said what was perhaps unthinkable just minutes before.

"I'm sorry to hear that, George."

George swallowed, clearly not expecting any sympathy from her.

"Thank you."

Jennifer was a leader and leaders had to have their team free from distraction and uncertainty. The next thing she offered she had not even run by Ochula beforehand.

"Laura," she gained Laura's attention with the sound of her voice. Laura looked up at her. "I got Jenny's pic off your HC. I don't know where she is. I've never met her. And I would never hurt her—I would never even try to find her to hurt her. I'm a bitch sometimes but I'm not in the habit of tracking down innocent people that are guilty of nothing more than association. I throttled you twice because you sold a weapon that hurt someone close to me. You didn't know the buyer. End of story. You can get up and leave any time you want."

Ochula sat back on the low couch glancing side-long at Laura to see what she was going to do. He wasn't surprised by Jennifer's admission. Jennifer had taken the lead that he had been following since minute one. It was her show.

Laura's eyes got moist but no tears formed. She just peered at Jennifer trying to determine what the good inside her was going to do with this new information.

"I'm still not certain that I want to help you. And I know I can't trust you." This was the only way a person like Laura knew how to respond. Even so, she did not get up and leave, although she was warming to the idea for sure.

Jennifer saw her last chance and went for it.

"Do you know why you have to wait until around 2am for George, Ochula, and I to hit Blanconales at *Rumors*, Laura?"

Laura had given the timing some thought. George had told her it would be well into the night before her part in the hit would be needed. That part was to make certain Jennifer's team had a guaranteed ingress into *Rumors* to hit Blanconales when he least expected it. That was it—letting Jennifer's team into the pleasure club by any means agreed upon was the complete extent of her role in all this.

Laura knew how to case a building and had done it before. She'd already started casing *Rumors* when she went for the interview. She was confident she could complete the task well before 2am. The thought did nag her—*Why DO they have to wait that long to hit Blanconales? I'll have the ingress ready well before then.*

Finally Laura's curiosity compelled her to ask the obvious. "Why?"

Jennifer took in a breath like she couldn't believe what she was going to say next.

"Because George, Ochula, and I are going to attempt to rescue all the people Blanconales has abducted from Sommerville. That's why."

Laura blinked. She turned to Ochula because he was the only person in the room she felt she could trust to confirm this outrageous claim.

Ochula's eyes had a mix of intense focus, readiness, and steely determination.

"That's right, Laura. So you see, your part may not even be needed."

"Not needed?"

Ochula's jaw set indicating his unbreakable will to complete this mission, no matter what the cost.

"I'm not certain that any of us will make it back to *Rumors* to take out Blanconales. If we don't show, just go home."

SIXTEEN

Laura *could* be counted on. What good she had inside her pushed her into doing the right thing, as did that her role was small and manageable. She worked with George, Ochula and Jennifer to plan how to provide an ingress to *Rumors,* then George and her left so that he could drop her off for the evening shift.

Laura had even come up with a unique way to get Jennifer's team into the pleasure club. She was given a sub-vocal mic and earbud then George took her to "work." Midnight on Beltina was 14 o'clock due to the 28-hour day. Her shift started at eight.

As soon as Laura left the suite, Jennifer rushed to the WC, fell to her knees, grabbed the porcelain god with both arms, and got sick.

That morning's non-event near the dead drop, being hammer slapped by George, and the stress of coercing Laura had caught up with her. Breathing hard, Jennifer pushed herself off the rim of the head, wiped at her mouth with a sleeve, then sat against the wall with one arm still draped over the toilet. Sweat dimpled her forehead from trying so hard to empty her gut. Her abdomen was on fire quivering with tiny uncontrollable spasms.

The pounding between Jennifer's ears was a resident succubus causing her eyes to bulge. Jennifer feared that no amount of medication would temper this episode, but dry swallowed two pills anyway nearly retching. The pills seem to land in her empty stomach like a bomb. She pulled her legs into her chest, wrapped her arms around them, and hugged herself hard hoping that it might help. It did...some. After a few minutes she leaned down slowly, careful to ease the side of her head gently atop her hand resting on the cold floor, then closed her eyes.

When Jennifer opened her bloodshot eyes, she didn't know where she was at first. Nothing new, she didn't know what time it was either. She tried to push up on her elbows to find out, then the pressure behind her forehead nixed that, so she collapsed back on the comfortable low couch. Her eyes shut and she drifted off somewhat peacefully.

The smell of food pulled Jennifer's eyes ajar. The light was low helping her open her flittering eyelids all the way. Her nausea was gone...somehow. When she swung her legs over the side of the low couch and sat up she saw why. On the coffee table in front of her was the open vial of Zofran pills. Her headache was distant, like an echo.

A hand touched her shoulder.

"I forced one down while you were sleeping." Ochula's voice soothed from behind her.

Jennifer twisted looking up at her friend.

"I'm a wreck, aren't I?"

Ochula came around the couch and sat down. He didn't fan the feeble fire Jennifer had started with the dry kindling of her chronic condition. Instead...

"I talked to Krachy. He said you really liked bacon, egg, and cheese whole grain tomato basil wraps. I found a cafe that let me talk them into making up a few." He smiled. His brow peaked. "You know, that milkshake we had earlier today was seven creds. Shame you had to waste it."

Jennifer's chin pitted pulling her mouth into a frown.

"Does Krachy know how sick I am?"

Ochula looked like he was a bit taken aback by the question, but tempered his reaction rather calmly as to not throw more fuel on the smoldering flames of her ill health.

"Nope."

"You know how to be a good leader, Ochula. You're not adding any distraction or uncertainty to what we have to do tonight."

"And…?"

"Maybe you should lead this team tonight."

"And…?"

"I don't think I'm up to it."

"And…? Go ahead, say it, Jennifer. You're not immune. Neither am I."

Jennifer gulped.

"I'm scared shitless that I'm going to screw up and leave Krachy alone."

Tears began a flowin', tumbling down her cheeks in little straight lines. The damn pills were making her maudlin and emotional—as usual.

After Jennifer sniffed for what seemed like the sixth time, Ochula reached over and brushed the new and drying tears from her cheeks with a napkin. He knew the other reason she was so upset was because of how sick she was getting.

"Better?" He asked trying to make light of it all.

Jennifer grunted, her body lifting with it. She licked her lips and rubbed at a spot on her cheek he'd missed.

"How about that food?" She stood up and went around the back of the low couch, then pulled out a chair at the table and sat down. She watched Ochula dig in the plasti provisions bag on the table and pull out a few wraps. She looked around the room as she unwrapped her food.

"Where's George?" Jennifer pushed the savory smelling grinder to her mouth forcing in a large bite.

Ochula sat down across from her and pushed a tall thermo mug of hot black coffee towards her. It was vacuum sealed so he had to thumb the lid release. The little lid flipped open.

"I told him you and I needed a few minutes. He's in the bedroom." His eyes glanced at the room behind Jennifer as he took a few sips of his own rich-smelling brew.

"Good call," Jennifer commented around a large mouthful. She swallowed and swigged carefully at the hot joe. "No need him seeing me like this."

"Like what?"

"Ochula, I know I'm a mess. You don't have to downplay it like that."

Ochula liked the sparkle in Jennifer's eyes when she snipped back at him.

She realized what he was doing.

"You and Krachy, stamping my buttons." She pushed a smile onto her lips, admitting to herself that she *was* starting to feel better. Mainly because Ochula was here to help.

"A little."

"A little what?"

"A little push is all you usually need. I'll point you in the right direction."

Jennifer knew where he was headed with this. Her wrap demolished, she covered a burp with her hand, eyeing the second one he'd gotten for her. After a few swigs of coffee to settle the first wrap calmly down inside her aching belly, she pulled the second one towards her pointing out thoughtfully, "We don't have a plan for actually extracting the horde of people at the holding site, do we? There's no way I can call in my ship *Viper II* to break orbit and help. Beltina Orb Control won't let a craft that big dirt-side without an approved flight plan. They'd shoot it out of the sky. Wouldn't they?"

"Yes, I believe they would."

Jennifer pointedly shook her head in a slow rhythm. This was obviously a distraction and an uncertain element of their plan. Worse still, she had no answer for it, so she turned the tables while taking a few bites.

"And…?"

"I should lead the team tonight."

"And…how does that solve the extraction problem?"

"Leave that to me."

"That's not an answer."

"You're not very good at blindly following orders, are you, Jen?"

"I'm distracted and uncertain, damn it! Help me with that!"

"George reconned the holding site with several floaters after he dropped Laura off. I took a hard look at that recon. I have a plan on how to handle the extraction. Besides, George has an impressive array of goodies being the arms dealer he is. Follow my lead this evening. Can you do that?"

Jennifer stopped chewing, ignoring his question and waiting for the payoff on how Ochula magically intended to solve this problem with words.

Ochula gave a smug look.

"Trust me."

***

Jennifer did trust Ochula—she always had. She could not have been happier that he was leading this foray tonight. The weight it pulled off her shoulders was huge.

Her illness was preventing her from solving such an immense yet simple problem: How can three people rescue so many people? While it was hard to push this dilemma aside, Jennifer had promised Ochula that she would follow his lead. With how bad her lingering episode from the hotel was, she wasn't fooling anyone about her ability to lead this operation successfully.

It occurred to Jennifer that she had worked herself into one of those labyrinths she had promised herself she would avoid. *What else am I missing?* If not for Ochula's confidence that the assault on the holding site would be a success, she would not have the courage to even try it.

Now all she had to do was concentrate on how to stay alive. And how to blindly follow orders. Which, admittedly, she was not very good at.

Jennifer burped and the smell of it filled the tight confines of the dura-armor commando suit helmet she was wearing. She'd used suits similar to this one, but never one this comfortable. This was the most advanced and intuitive piece of attack gear she had ever draped over her body. George certainly did have access to a resplendent array of high-tech armaments.

Carefree about the protection surrounding her body, Jennifer could now focus on how to be a subordinate. The next thing she said was an attempt to let Ochula know that the underling role she'd agreed to play fit just right.

"Every hunter needs a good guide," she remarked to Ochula with mild enthusiasm. He was sitting in the passenger seat of George's air car. George was behind the controls driving the air car with Jennifer in back. They all had on similar dura-armor suits.

"Don't patronize me, Bane," Ochula admonished, fighting to get out the words past a yawn. He hadn't been able to grab a nap like Jennifer.

"You're all rested and frisky," crackled back over the commo in her helmet.

Jennifer's face bent into a smile she didn't feel as she continued to worry about how this evening's labyrinth would unfold.

George parked the air car off the road behind a stand of trees about a mile from the holding site. The route he'd navigated to bring them this close was one of the less traveled air car roads leading to the north side of the holding site. Sommerville was to the south.

The three of them got out of the air car and formed up in front of the hood. Their visors flipped up one after another. Jennifer pushed her loaded bum bag around her waist centering it on her left hip for easy access if needed. During the air car ride, she'd had it swiveled around in front so that she could sit in back without it jabbing her lower back against the seat.

Ochula took control, his voice steady and decisive.

"We're a mile away. We're going to head due south and come up behind the large main building. Our Anti Grav Harnesses will be able to traverse the rough terrain at a good ground-eating pace. It should only take us five minutes before the site comes into view."

Jennifer held her tongue and for the first time realized what Ochula was doing. He was feeding her what she needed to know and nothing more. It dawned on Jennifer that she was now a weapon. A weapon that needed to be aimed. Aimed at what Ochula deemed a target.

Instead of questioning Ochula, Jennifer started to check the load on her weapon, the one that she would soon be aiming. She unslung the laser pulse rifle and racked the slide on the mag boomer launcher tucked up under the barrel. She'd never used one of these before but it looked well designed and simple.

Ochula was watching her look over the stubby underside of the mag launcher. He reached over and grabbed it.

"All right," Ochula said. He demonstrated the safety above the trigger.

"This has a 20-round magazine. The slide has to be racked each time. It'll recoil some and can only be used for close quarters combat. The small magnetic boomer punches out and will stick to anything metal. Once attached, the delay is one second. The shaped charge of the boomer is forward facing, it'll detonate away from you and into the person or object it's stuck to. Got it?" He handed it back over to Jennifer.

"Why am I the only one carrying one?" Jennifer asked.

"Easy to reload for a novice, and you'll need the shorter length in close quarters," Ochula explained. "I need you to secure the small building, Jennifer. George and I are going to handle the main building."

This was the first bit of detailed direction Jennifer received. Her burning curiosity could not, however, be contained any longer.

"How are you going to extract ALL the people that are being held in the main building, Ochula?"

He ignored her, continuing his instructions. George listened intently.

"Use the sights for the laser rifle only, Jennifer. The laser rifle atop the launcher is just like the ones you've used before. The mag boomer only travels 20 or 30 feet before projectile drop, so the sight is useless for it. You can fire the launcher from your hip which helps manage the recoil. Get close to your target and let it fly. Remember the one-second delay."

Ochula addressed them both.

"The AGHs are quiet. We'll swing around the far side of the perimeter looking for an unlit corner on the north side of the main building. George and I will go in. Jennifer, you cover us if things get nasty. Once George and I gain access to the main building, you hit the small one."

Ochula drilled Jennifer with a glare.

"I'm not going to lie to you. This is going to be a serious gamble. George's recon uncovered a strategy that I intend to exploit. I'm betting our lives and the lives of anyone inside that I'm right."

Jennifer's heart began beating faster pushing the hooded daze from her head that lingered after the meds she'd taken earlier. She could see why Ochula was the head of Markem's military. The iron in his voice drove people to follow him— and to not let him down while they did.

He must have a plan to liberate all the abducted people. Maybe there are several air buses in the main building large enough to transport them all?

George spoke for the first time.

"Jennifer, don't hit any power sources on the outside of either buildings. In fact, don't hit any power sources at all," he advised.

Jennifer didn't understand why, but when she looked at Ochula's eyes, they narrowed in confirmation.

"I understand. I'll cover you both then hit the small building. If there are people in there that need to be rescued, I'll ingress into the main building and usher them in if I can." Jennifer eyeballed Ochula for another confirmation.

Ochula gave her a nod of approval taking her statement as fact.

The three of them were no longer ordinary people driven by ordinary circumstances—they were compelled to make a difference now.

George saw the realization assemble behind Jennifer's eyes.

She turned to him.

"This is what you wanted, George. Make it count."

"Thank you."

She knew what he meant.

Jennifer pushed at the joypad in her glove with a finger to guide her AGH toward the position she'd chosen to cover Ochula and George. She was fifty yards behind them as they approached the darkened west corner of the main building. She floated five feet above the ground sliding through the shadows of deep night slowly, but easily, to avoid getting too close as to not have a wide view of the back of the large main building.

She spotted motion out of the corner of her eye. She lowered herself to the ground, cutting the power on her AGH, so she could take up a shooting stance on one knee. Her instincts had guided her through the darkness bringing her to a threat that was easily anticipated—a lone sentry rounding the east corner of the building.

Jennifer took in a deep, quiet breath, pumping oxygen into her system, and shouldered her pulse rifle. She tugged the trigger lancing a spark of energy through the darkness. The bolt bulldozed into the sentry's mouth slamming him backwards to the ground like a cut tree.

With George at his heels, Ochula cut the power on his AGH planting his feet on the ground, knees pumping at a slow jog. He crept the last twenty feet to the main building's west corner, his flechette rifle leading the way, when he heard Jennifer's voice in his ear.

"Sentry down east of your position."

"Copy that," Ochula replied.

Jennifer began moving slowly toward the west corner of the holding site to provide more cover and to make her way to the small building located further down that side of the facility. The servos in her suit whined rhythmically with each measured step. She vocalized a command to bring up the infrared scanner on her visor and did a quick scan of the motionless sentry. The hands and head of the dead sentry were light yellow, the rest of his body dark blue. In IR, the hottest objects were represented by brighter colors, white or yellow, while cooler objects were represented by darker colors, blue or black.

He must have on dura-armor arm and leg wraps with a vest around his torso. If the other sentries have on similar protection my mag boomer will stick to their armor.

Jennifer continued to keep moving while scanning the backside of the large metal structure. Her brows bunched stopping on an intensely bright spot in the center of the 150-foot-wide back wall at ground level.

The white hot blotch was maybe seven-foot-high and three-feet-wide with a laser sharp yellow outline encircling it.

The hell is that?

The object was inside the building putting out enough energy to paint a fierce shimmering glow through the back wall of the holding site.

Maybe that's why George told me not to hit any power sources.

Distracted by the odd discovery, Jennifer cursed herself for losing track of Ochula and George's progress. They had disappeared like ghosts into the shadows around the west corner of the building.

Before Jennifer could chastise herself further, the commo in her suit crackled.

"Keep up, Bane!" Ochula snapped sharply.

Fully aware of the consequences of a screwup, Jennifer tried to banish her confusion so that she could be focused in the moment. She had to fight to clear the eeriness of the white blotch discovery from her head.

Nothing else is gonna distract me.

"Copy that," Jennifer acknowledged, already jogging quickly around the west corner concentrating on the two bobbing blue figures ahead. Her IR tracked the up-and-down footsteps of the barely discernible heat emissions from Ochula's and George's commando suits in front of her.

Jennifer's attempt to stay focused was failing. Her peripheral vision kept catching fleeting glimpses of the white blotch getting brighter and brighter as she moved down the length of the west side of the building.

Ochula and George had stopped up ahead. They were between the large building on their left and the small building on their right.

Jennifer caught up to them turning a full 180 degrees to check her six while Ochula worked the scan pad next to the entry hatch to the holding site. She didn't see what Ochula did to make the hatch unlock so easily, but heard the confirm in her ear.

"We're going in. Here, take this," Ochula instructed.

Jennifer wheeled around reaching for the scan pad overlay device in Ochula's outstretched gloved hand. She took it.

Ochula instructed fast.

"Slap it on the scan pad next to the hatch on the small building and hit the actuator. The computer will do the rest." With that, he passed a hand in front of the scan pad opening the hatch, then he and George rushed into the dark confines of the cavernous holding site. The hatch snapped shut behind them.

Jennifer cut the IR on her visor. She turned to step over to the hatch leading into the small building not eight feet away, then heard the sharp, wicked sounds of rapid-fire flechette darts piercing the air over the enhance microphone in her suit.

Thift-thift-thift-thift-thift-thift chattered then stopped abruptly, starting again, in random, agitated bursts. Ochula and George were in a fire fight inside the holding site!

Jennifer pushed the overlay device she'd been given against the scan pad next to the small building hatch. It snapped against the flat pad with a magnetic click. She pressed the toggle switch on the top corner—nothing happened. She fingered the switch again—nothing, a third time—zilch.

The intermittent bursts of prattling dart fire, sharp and distinct in her ears over the suit's enhanced mic, was becoming a distraction. As was the fact that this stupid, and now obviously useless, *hatch opener* was NOT going to work.

The soundless lull of dart fire from the holding site allowed Jennifer to recognize the sound of two guards rounding the south corner of the holding site behind her. Jennifer spun around punching out a mag boomer from the launcher. The stubby barrel coughed a distinctive sound as the small magnetic projectile impacted the armored vest of the first sentry.

Onn-weep—clank.

The mag launcher sounded slamming the mag boomer into the guard's stomach pushing him backwards into the second guard behind him.

A second later the shaped charge exploded in a boiling, tight, v-shaped tunnel of destruction boring through the guard's belly. The messy discharge of bloody fluids sprayed the stunned guard behind him. The lifeless corpse collapsed in a puddle.

Jennifer had already racked the mag launcher slide and propelled one, then racked and fired another boomer at the remaining sentry.

Onn-weep—clank. Onn-weep—clank.

The two boomers hit home side-by-side across the guard's abdomen, jerking him backwards a few paces, then exploded.

The two charges detonated in rapid succession stopping the sentry forever, slicing his torso in half. The lacerated top-half of the body toppled forward, the bottom-half backward to the ground.

Jennifer turned back to the confounded small building hatch that would not open and decided to use the tool that she knew WOULD open it.

Onn-weep—clank.

The boomer exploded a second later through the hatch. The jagged hole was large enough for Jennifer to stick her armored arm through to reach inside. She leaned in and passed her gloved hand over the scan pad inside the room next to the hatch. It moved aside.

Just then an alert flashed up on her visor. The red alert read, *Chlorine Gas.*

Before she could process the warning, her suit auto-sealed itself hermetically. Every gap in the suit that would allow air inside sealed with an air-tight *hawhipp.* Jennifer's ears popped then she saw the green mist in the dim-lit room rolling down through vents in the ceiling like hazy fog.

There was an aisle down the center of the 20-foot by 20-foot room. On either side of the aisle were curtains hung up by wires, four curtains on each side. What was behind each curtain was not clear. Jennifer flipped on the IR in her visor and scanned the room spotting heat sources behind each curtain on both sides. The shapes were people! Reclined people, in what had to be low beds or cots.

I've gotta get them out!

Jennifer lunged right grabbing the first flimsy curtain she could reach pulling it aside. The suit's headlamp flipped on. The beam of light landed on the agonized face of a naked young woman gasping to pull in a breath free from the poison. Her terrified eyes landed on Jennifer.

Jennifer's heart skipped, her face mutating into an aghast expression of recognition and God help her soul—regret.

The woman was Laura Measures' partner—Jenny.

SEVENTEEN

Jennifer knew she couldn't close her mind entirely on the outrage coursing through her boiling veins. But she tried. She had to. She had to save Jenny and all the people being poisoned by the chlorine gas.

She moved suddenly, darting forward scooping up Jenny easily with servo driven arms. She retreated fast out the hatch turning left and deposited Jenny as gently as she could on the ground just past the north corner of the small building. Jennifer made repeated trips back into the room rescuing woman after woman. There were no men to rescue.

The quiet respite of dart fire from the main building was interrupted by Ochula's voice in Jennifer's ear.

"Holding site secure."

Jennifer had pulled the last of the naked women from the small building and was now bent down over Jenny. Laura's partner was coughing uncontrollably struggling to pull enough air into her chest to expel another wheezing hack.

Jennifer's heart raced in her chest as she looked into the watery red eyes of the woman she had promised Laura she would not harm. Her only thought was how to save her life.

"Ochula!" She barked into her suit mic. "I need help out here! Eight people from the small building have been poisoned. Help me!"

"Negative," came the response in her helmet.

Jennifer's eyes hardened and narrowed into slits as she watched Jenny fighting for her life. She couldn't believe Ochula wouldn't help. She leapt up, turned, and ran over to the entry hatch to the main building. Her arm rocketed down past the scan pad and the hatch rushed aside. She jumped into the huge building past the threshold then stopped in her tracks.

Down the periphery of the building's walls were metal shelves jutting out. The shelves were at least fifty feet deep and stacked five high. Metal ladders were spaced uniformly on the front of the shelves that allowed the people to climb into the gaps between each shelf. The shelves encircled nearly the entire perimeter of the holding site except for what looked like a WC and small galley area. Jennifer took several frantic steps forward to see what was in the center of the room.

The center of the room was a large square area that held one object. Ochula was to the right of the seven-foot-high, three-feet-wide stand-alone doorway with his back to Jennifer. He led another person toward it, then the person stepped through into the glistening white brilliance and disappeared in a spark of light. Ochula was directing the hundreds of people that were making their way down the ladders from the shelving bunks into the portal. George was directing traffic instructing the abducted people to climb down from their berthing shelves and line up to be ushered through the gate.

Jennifer shook off her confusion and ran toward Ochula. She had to sidestep at least four fallen guards lying on the deck behind him. She came to a rushing halt just as he turned.

Ochula's face was contorted with a rage of its own.

"Help George! Get the rest of these people to the Coupling Gate!" He ordered.

"But I have peopled outside dyin—"

Ochula interrupted.

"—You only have eight people out there! I have at least fourteen-hundred-and-fifty in here. Do the math! Help George! NOW!" He screamed leaving no room for dissent.

Jennifer did as she was ordered all the while picturing Jenny and the others with their lungs on fire fighting to stay alive now that she had abandoned them. As Jennifer escorted group after group of abducted people toward the gate, her anger began to rise despite all the lives she was helping to save.

An injured holding site guard struggled to stand up. None of the abducted people, for obvious reasons, offered to help him. He gripped one of the shelve support columns. The man used his good arm to pull himself standing.

Jennifer spotted him, her fists clinched around her rifle, and rolled her shoulders back, glaring at the guard. She was going to exact revenge for Jenny, for all of the victims she was not allowed to help. In her mind, Jennifer was growing larger and larger, expanding with rage.

If I don't kill him, fast, to get myself under control, I'll explode and take out everyone around me.

Jennifer lifted the pulse rifle high, stepped up to the scared man, tensing her arms to smash the butt of the weapon into the guard's forehead.

George appeared in front of her shooting his hands up to grab the weapon before it could descend. His eyes pinned Jennifer's eyes.

"Back off! Right. Now."

George had compassion for life, any life, and intended to save the guard. He would not allow Jennifer to act.

The disdain in Jennifer's eyes could have melted dura-lead. But George was unwavering. His fierce grip ahold her rifle was vice-like.

Jennifer retreated to her duties. After what had to be fifteen minutes, the last of the abducted peopled blinked through the Coupling Gate. Transported off to somewhere that Jennifer didn't even know the location of.

Ochula had planned the extraction through THE gate. It was obvious. The head of Markem's military had access to technology that Jennifer knew nothing about. But Ochula knew. And he and George had planned the rescue without her. The revelation that she'd been purposefully left out was NOT as severe as the revelation that hit Jennifer when she retreated out of the main building. Jennifer came to a stop looking down at the gas victims.

All eight women were dead.

Jennifer eased her powered arms under Jenny's breathless corpse and flipped on her AGH lifting them both off the ground. She didn't care what Ochula and George did. She was going to bring Jenny with her. Jennifer couldn't picture her life, her future, if she left this poor, helpless, fallen innocent woman behind.

Jennifer arrived at the air car dropping herself to the ground next to the back door on the driver's side. With one outstretched finger she tapped the small entry pad on the door handle. The door lifted up and back. Jennifer eased herself into the back seat carefully with Jenny's body in her arms. Doing so with the powered suit took no thought. That was good. Very good. Jennifer didn't want to think. Maybe ever again. Her eyes landed on Jenny's pale face. Jenny's head rested in Jennifer's lap. She reached over and pulled Jenny's legs into the back seat so that the door could be closed when the time came.

Despite the attempt to clear her mind, Jennifer agonized over one chilling thought: *How am I ever going to face Laura again..?*

***

George drove the air car in silence with Ochula in the passenger seat. Jennifer sat brooding in the back seat with Jenny growing ever colder in her lap.

Ochula turned, his visor up and sweat dripping from his brows.

"The Coupling Gate was being used to relocate abduction victims, Jennifer."

Jennifer searched her friend's face. A face that had been so caring earlier in the evening back at the hotel suite. But now that face had the weight of grim decision etched across it. Hard decisions and hard choices. Choices that had been forced on her. Jennifer saw *the leader's dilemma* behind Ochula's eyes. She had made a similar choice when she first started this mission—protect the many and expose the one. In her case, the one was Krachy. In Ochula's case, the one was Jenny.

"Why were there so many people, Ochula?" Jennifer just couldn't understand how that many people could have been abducted from Sommerville.

George answered.

"I pointed out that you weren't asking the right question, Jennifer. You didn't ask WHEN? The other question that you and Ochula didn't ask was HOW MANY? The holding site was too big to house abducted people from just Sommerville. The holding site held all the abducted people from every city on the planet. That's why it was so big. The Coupling Gate was transporting people from every city on the planet to be housed in that one location." George eased the air car around a wide turn heading in the direction of Sommerville and the pleasure club.

Jennifer looked at Ochula.

"That's right, Jennifer. When George did his recon after dropping Laura off, he captured the IR image of the heat bloom generated by the Coupling Gate.

"In all the time since the cease-fire with Beltina, I've had my OWN scientists on Markem trying to develop a transporting Receiver just like Beltina's. We couldn't do it. We've been unable to develop such a large spaceship transportation device. We couldn't get the immense power source solved to transport such large objects through hyperspace. But what my team DID do, was develop a transporter that could send people through hyperspace one person at a time. I sent every one of the abducted people that were at the holding site back to Markem. We rescued over fourteen-hundred-and-fifty hostages just now.

"Do you see now why it was so important to save the people that could be saved, Jennifer?" Ochula's eyes framed Jennifer's hoping for a reprieve for the choice he had to make.

Jennifer was silent.

Ochula kept trying.

"The prime minister was using a modified version of the large Receiver that your vassal Jeffrey Jansen runs. Blanconales and his scientists have scaled down the Receiver. The Coupling Gate you saw was that scaled down version. Similar gates have been installed all over the planet in discreet locations. When people are abducted by fake first responders, they are taken to the gate near the city they're from, then relocated to Sommerville's holding site. Every city on Beltina relocates their victims to the holding site we just shut down."

"But you never told me, Ochula. You didn't trust me!" Jennifer glanced down at Jenny then back at Ochula, her cheeks reddening. Laura would never trust her either. Jennifer'd be lucky if Laura didn't try to kill her now that Jenny was dead.

"I made an educated guess after I took a hard look at George's intel. It wasn't until George and I breached the holding site that I knew I was right."

He wiped at his face a few times with a hand pulling sweat away.

"Jennifer, I needed your help. You covered us while we hit the main building. I knew I couldn't let you lead this team tonight. Not only are you not physically up to it, you would have saved the few, and not the many." He shook his head. "I had to get all those people safe. Don't you understand?"

"You mean you knew Jenny was going to be in the small building. You talk like you know everything."

"Of course I didn't know that, Jennifer. I needed to give you a task you could handle. You've always proved to be a reliable piece of ordinance when properly motivated...like tonight. I needed you to chin people and I knew I could count on you to do just that. You bought us time. It wasn't your fault the small building was booby trapped with poisonous gas."

"Why were the women even in there? It looked like they were being held there, in the small building, then if they tried to escape, the gas was released."

Ochula looked over at George as if he was trying to get a confirmation that he should tell Jennifer the truth.

Jennifer looked at George then back at Ochula.

Ochula blinked, letting out a slow breath, coming to what seemed like yet another hard decision. That decision was going to upset Jennifer even more.

"I looked in the small building, Jennifer. I don't want to tell you what I saw and what you didn't. Can't you wait until after the night is over to get into that?"

"I saw eight young women behind curtain—" Her breath caught.

Ochula continued reluctantly. There was no way Jennifer would let it go and he knew it.

"Above each curtain was a number. Numbers 1 through 8. Men like Blanconales. Men like his friends. Men that craved a diversion were given a number, went behind that curtain, then defiled the woman lying in the bed. It was set up as a rape rally, Jennifer. Nothing short of what slavers do by human trafficking women. Blanconales segregated the most desirable women that were abducted and sent them to the small building. The gas was there to prevent them from telling anyone if the small building was broken into. The gas would eliminate any witnesses."

Ochula finally had to say what needed to be said. What a leader had to assess when applying the devastating burden of *the leader's dilemma* to the mission.

"Jennifer, when I refused to help you, I knew you'd come storming into the holding site. I needed your help to get the people that had the best chance to live through the gate fast. Once you said poison, I had to make a decision. I didn't know how long the power would stay up to keep the gate functional. I also didn't know how long the women you found would stay alive if they stayed alive at all. So I traded those women for the many. I'm not proud about what I did. I'm only proud of what I didn't do: I didn't let over fourteen-hundred-and-fifty people die. I punched in the coordinates of the Coupling Gate I had constructed on Markem and sent all the abducted people through hyperspace to save them."

Jennifer looked away trying to collect herself then finally looked down at Jenny's dead body again. Her lifeless open eyes had turned opaque and cloudy. Jennifer would never know the impact Jenny may have had on her life. The crushing weight of responsibility seemed to transfer slowly from Jenny into Jennifer with each passing moment. The more Jenny dehydrated and grew smaller, the more Jennifer expanded with guilt.

George guided the air car into Sommerville. *Rumors* was located in an elegant, tree-lined area between an art museum and a hip restaurant. The immediate neighborhood had chic galleries and hair boutiques, all bracketed east and west by nameless streets, more like alleys, leading around to the back of the club on either side.

To the north of *Rumors*, the direction George chose to approach the club, was a construction site.

Ochula thought it was a good vantage point for Jennifer to set up to watch the front entrance.

"Jennifer?" He tried to get her attention.

When Jennifer's head lifted from staring at Jenny her eyes were blood shot.

"George is going to pull around the back of the construction site. We're going to let you out so you can watch the front entrance. If Blanconales alludes George, he may come out the front. If that happens you need to drop him. You understand?"

"Ochula, I can't leave Jenny exposed while we do this. I know she doesn't care now but I do."

Along with her concern for leaving Jenny's unconcealed body in the back seat, Jennifer was momentarily confused. Ochula told her to drop Blanconales if he alluded George.

Why didn't Ochula say if Blanconales alludes us—both he and George?

George's next statement cut into Jennifer's uncertainty.

"I covered the weapons in the boot with a blanket, Jennifer. I'll get it when we drop you off."

George concentrated on bringing the air car to a stop in the deserted alley behind the construction site. He jumped out. Jennifer heard the boot open then close. At the same time Ochula got out quickly passing in front of the air car to get in behind the controls. The driver side back door opened and George draped the dark blue blanket over Jenny, tenderly tucking it around and under her as if to make her more comfortable. If not for the softly whining servos in his suit, what he just did would have been completely silent with what seemed like reverence. He looked into Jennifer's eyes.

"Is that okay?" He asked letting Jennifer decide if his work was acceptable or not.

Jennifer nodded. She could tell what he'd just done was for her and not Jenny.

"Yes."

George dipped his head somberly, pushed the door closed, hurried around the back of the air car, then slid into the passenger seat.

EIGHTEEN

An icy spike went straight down Laura Measures' back when the Fixer at *Rumors* asked her about employment references. Laura was in his small office off the lobby sitting in the lone chair in front of his desk legs uncrossed. With sunglasses still on her eyes, she was easily adjusting to the office's bright light. The time was just past 1am, and up until a few minutes ago, Laura had been given free run of the club. She didn't expect to be asked about references and hadn't covered this contingency with Ochula, Jennifer, and George back at the hotel suite.

The Fixer had pulled her aside and insisted she follow him to his office. Laura thought the perv just wanted to get another few eye fulls of her body, but that was not the case. She had misread the Fixer's intentions. All things considered, not a complete surprise. Laura wasn't good at reading men. Her real skill was to perform in front of them…not to get close and understand them. She would just have to wing it…

Just as Laura was about to answer the Fixer with some lame-ass excuse why she didn't have any references, two things happened. The tiny ear bud in her right ear crackled to life and the pocket door to the office moved aside.

The club hostess stepped into the room past the threshold. She was a young rail-thin black lady with a shaved head half covered with a purple silk head scarf that ran loosely down around her neck, high cheek bones that seemed to glisten and reflect light off them, and wide full lips. She wore a long-sleeved purple latex skin suit, but no shoes—she was barefoot. Every raw-boned skeletal protuberance on her body was visible under the sheen slick bodysuit, including the camel toe between her legs that looked strangely beefy and out of place on such a gaunt physique.

The lighting in the pleasure club was so low, especially with the shades on, Laura hadn't noticed the hostess's moose knuckle until now.

Damn, if she'd feed that thing a normal pair of trousers, instead of that bodysuit, it wouldn't munch on her like that, Laura postulated to herself.

Laura didn't hear the voice in her earbud, or the question the Fixer asked again. She was preoccupied staring at the woman's taco.

"LAURA!!" George shrilled in her ear, pulling her dreamy gaze from the fine view of the hostess's frontal wedgie.

Laura blinked her attention back to the Fixer. The man was in his fifties with a hefty paunch that sloshed over his belt almost touching his thighs as he sat. The man had a full fake head of black hair poorly fitted on top of an obviously bald head. His gray eyebrows didn't match the rug. Why in the world he wore a white spandex too-small-for-his-body short-sleeved shirt was a mystery. His blubbery torso looked like a stuffed sausage forced into the sprayed on shirt.

Laura couldn't respond to the loud rasp in her ear from George without giving herself away.

"Tell the Fixer that your references are the three third place finishes in the Ms. Beltina competition. He just asked you!" George scolded, obviously hearing the question the Fixer asked even though Laura hadn't. The sub-vocal mic on her throat worked fine.

"I came in third three times in the Ms. Beltina competition. You can pull that up on your hand comp." She leaned forward grabbing the Fixer's hand comp that was on the desk and made a show of handing it to him. As she did, her legs opened tugging her skirt toward her waist revealing her clam shell in all its man's-best-friend glory. She sat back keeping her legs open.

The Fixer's eyes consumed what was in front of him. He then looked up at Laura's face, a ripple of uncertainty passing across his features.

"You understand I just need to make sure you're on the level. I mean it's part of our hiring process." He cleared his throat.

Laura inched her legs open more causing the lips between her hips to part languidly.

"Take your time." She smiled.

Even the hostess did a double-take on Laura's prize. She returned her attention to the Fixer as he pecked at the HC screen retrieving the information.

"The prime minister's bodyguards are creeping out some of the clients."

The Fixer wasn't all that good a multitasking. He continued fingering the HC screen getting close to what he was looking for.

The hostess's jaw clenched.

"Jon, did you hear what I just said? The two guys skulking next to the entrance to the pleasure rooms are making people nervous. Not everyone, but some." She began drumming her foot.

Jon looked up at her.

"So? What do you want me to tell them? Leave? The PM gets whatever he wants when he's here, Shawna."

Shawna grunted not having it.

"But no one can use one of the pleasure rooms while his two guards flank the entrance. Blanconales doesn't need six rooms all to himself. As a matter of fact, he hasn't even asked for a companion or a pleasure droid since he went back there."

Jon nodded slowly letting that information sink in.

Then he asked.

"He's back there all by himself?"

She paused and caught Jon's eyes.

"Yes."

Jon thought some more about that but was nonplussed.

"The whole point of coming here is privacy. You know that. If the PM wants privacy to do whatever he's doing, then we just have to give it to him. The rooms back there are soundproofed for a reason." He finished his speech with mild conviction. The prime minister had visited the club many times in the past but had never behaved like this.

Jon returned his attention to Laura.

"Three thirds in three years. Impressive." He sat the hand comp off to the side. "I guess that's as good as a formal reference." He gave a glad eye to her parted legs briefly. "So everything going okay so far, Laura?"

Shawna didn't like not getting her way but said nothing further. When she turned on a foot, it squeaked against the slick floor. Her hand passed down over the scan pad and the door moved out of her way. She stepped out into the dark lobby.

Laura stood up.

"Fine, Jon. You want me to talk with the two guys Shawna mentioned? I can try to make their evening more relaxing even though it sounds like they can't leave their post or whatever."

Jon considered that for a moment.

"Check with Shawna first. She's in charge of the club floor."

Laura dipped her head, pulled down her skirt with aplomb, then swept out of the office enveloped by the shadows on the other side of the doorway.

Jon hungrily watched her backside leave last.

Out in the dark lobby Laura approached Shawna. What she had just heard about what the prime minister was doing worried her on several levels. First, the ingress that Laura had cased earlier depended on having access to the pleasure rooms. There was a hallway leading to the six pleasure rooms. All six rooms were lined down the right side of that hallway that dead ended at an emergency exit door—the door at the end of the hallway. It was this door that Laura wanted to use to let Ochula, George, and Jennifer into the club. Second, if the PM was alone he wasn't distracted or otherwise being "entertained." If Blanconales wasn't pre-occupied, he may be able to receive incoming comms that would alert him to what had taken place at the holding site.

Shawna was standing off to one side of the wide entryway looking into the main room when Laura stopped behind her. The way Shawna surveyed the main room made it clear her eyes were trying to adapt to the low light after being in Jon's bright office. Laura too was squinting and blinking waiting for her pupils to grow so she could see better. She'd pull off her sunglasses if it wouldn't reveal her injured eye. There was only so much adjusting her eyes could do with them on.

The faint tone of soothing chill music vibes drifted out of the main room. Laura waited another full ten seconds to get more of her night vision back before she tapped Shawna on the shoulder.

Shawna turned at the touch.

"Nice performance back there. You had Jon eating from the trough so to speak." She crossed her arms.

"I didn't have an answer for the references at first. I really need the extra creds this job provides, so I mentioned the most important things I've ever accomplished. I'm glad it was enough."

Shawna casually watched a servo droid pass by heading into the main room then looked back at her reflection in Laura's sunglasses. She uncrossed her arms.

"You like women don't you?" There it was. Trying to hide anything from this lady would be pointless.

"I do," Laura admitted.

Shawna cracked a half smile and emotion flashed in her eyes for a millisecond. It could have been anger from hearing her honest answer or intrigue over asking such an obvious question—obvious to her that is. Or both.

"What are you going to do when one of the clients ramps things up? You going to break the man's arm if he touches your hotspot? Looks like you could do that easily."

Laura knew where Shawna was going with this. The hostess of *Rumors* could not have one of their clients thumped and expect to stay in business. Laura answered the only way she knew how given her background and proclivities. The thought of letting down Jenny had to be pushed aside for the moment. Laura did not know that her partner was already dead.

I apologize my love…

"I'm okay with letting a client take what he needs from me. I wouldn't be here if I wasn't. Afterwards we could find a safe space alone so I can show you my appreciation."

Shawna took a long toe-to-head inspection of Laura and at the end her lips tightened.

"I'm flattered. Thank you. But I can't allow myself to get involved with staff. I like my work and want to keep things professional."

Laura's tinted lenses never left Shawna's eyes.

"You can't blame me for trying." The thought of cheating on Jenny sickened Laura but the sentiment didn't register on her face. Instead, she noticed that her eyes were seeing the dim purple-blueish light in the main room better now. She darted a look toward the two men standing on either side of the pleasure room entrance over thirty feet away.

"Jon told me to check with you before I had a chat with the guards." Her brows hiked.

"That's fine. But if another client asks for you to sit with them, I'm going to pull you away." The tone of Shawna's response made it clear she was moving past the rebuff and to establish the fact that business is business and she was in charge of that business.

Laura turned and started making her way toward the guards. When she was far enough away from Shawna she said lowly into the sub-vocal mic, "The PM is alone in one of the pleasure rooms. The ingress at the end of that hallway is compromised."

While receiving a confirm in her ear from George, and not from Ochula for some reason, her knee accidentally bumped the side of one of the bio couches. The dark alcove where it was positioned on the right wall made it very hard to see—but not hear. The man using the Aperture Option on the interactive couch seemed to be enjoying himself immensely. The female companion positioned behind him used two hands, one on each hip, to guide his lunging stiffy into the happy crack created by the automated love seat.

A waist-high sani droid rolled to a halt a few feet from the couch waiting for the man to finish so it could sanitize and disinfect.

Laura side-stepped the droid careful not to bump into a low table in front of a few chairs unoccupied at the moment. She came to a halt in front of the two guards.

The guard on the right was a tall, muscular man. He took a step toward her with the self-confidence of an athlete, obviously aware of his commanding presence. His hair was thick and brown, and his tanned face was deeply lined. His eye whites studied Laura. She couldn't see his dark pupils. If there was a flaw in his appearance, it was his hooked nose that seemed to point down at her exuding a threat of ruthless cruelty.

Hook Nose spoke up instantly.

"Come with me."

Before Laura had a chance flash a fake smile, Hook Nose clamped his strong hand around her bicep and pulled. Laura thought about resisting out of instinct. She hated when men touched her. That impulse quickly faded, however, when the other short guard rammed a laser pistol into the small of her back giving her no chance to retreat.

A surge of alarm bells went off in Laura's head.

Not good! Not good!

Hook Nose and Short Guy forcefully led Laura through the pleasure room entrance pulling the pocket door closed behind them.

Hook Nose rose a finger to his lips and shook his head twice making his point clear.

Short Guy roughly clamped a tie wrap around Laura's wrists like a vice then shot a hand through both elbows, pinning their boney points against his chest in a practiced move. For good measure, he sank his thumb painfully into the Brachii Trigger Point just under her left bicep. Nerve-shattering volts of searing numbness and eye-blinking pain rifled through the entire left side of Laura's body and face.

Hook Nose carefully reached under the choker on Laura's neck pulling off the sub-vocal mic. Another finger reached in her ear plinking out the flesh-colored ear bud.

Hook Nose's smile was void of human compassion.

As Laura was painfully led down the hall toward a pleasure room, she realized what Ochula had hoped to accomplish was about to fall apart. Lad Blanconales knew she was a plant. It didn't help that Laura had just started work tonight. All the signs that she was an *agent-up-to-no-good* were too numerous for the PM to ignore. Laura quickly figured out that she was probably going to die.

Jenny, my love, I'm sorry for leaving you...

NINETEEN

Listening to Laura's progress inside the club, Jennifer was both pleased and concerned from her vantage point looking down at the entrance from across the street. Pleased that Laura, the club hostess, and the Fixer, were on agreeable terms. Terms that allowed Laura to pinpoint the position of Lad Blanconales in one of the pleasure rooms. Two guards or not, at least Jennifer knew where the prime minister was. But concerned that it had been a full ten minutes since Laura went off-line. The sub-vocal mic had gone silent just when intel was needed the most. Jennifer also hated that Laura was in such close proximity to a man like Blanconales.

More disturbingly, to the point that Jennifer's heart felt like it was palpitating, Ochula had not checked-in *once* since they had parted ways in the alley behind the construction site. Jennifer's alarm at the cavalcade of bad and ever-expanding set of anomalies was pushing her into a panic attack. Jennifer had never had one before but for some reason knew what was happening.

The fact that Jennifer's health was declining at a frightening rate was an underlying gloom cradling her every jittery thought and sense. She could not separate this mission from her ill health. The mind was a powerful enemy when allowed to feed one's indecision. Right now Jennifer's mind was her enemy—not the PM.

This snowballing apprehension was making Jennifer sweat inside her dura-armor suit.

Where the hell is Ochula?! How am I going to explain Jenny's death to Laura? What's she going to do to me when I do?! Should I comm George to get a sit rep? If I break radio silence will I get everyone killed? And now I'm getting claustrophobic inside this damn suit!

Shit! I can't TAKE THIS ANYMORE!!

Jennifer shot to her feet, dropped her laser pulse rifle, then vocalized the command.

"Extract!"

The seam on both shoulders popped apart splitting open like a clam shell. The breach grew in a straight line down each arm until the front and back halves of the suit allowed Jennifer to pull out her arms, then reach up and remove her helmet, which she dropped on the deck. She looked up, saw an exposed durasteel I beam, jumped up and grabbed it suspending her weight. She pulled both legs out of the rigid self-standing suit, then used both feet to kick it out of her way so she could jump back down onto the deck.

Her tension retreated somewhat, finally free from the confines of her prison. Bending down, she unclipped the bum bag from around the waist of the inert suit, stood up, and cinched it around her waist adjusting the cordura belt so it fit snugly. She bent and grabbed the pulse rifle, sliding her arm through the sling, then made her way to the stairwell in the corner of the unfinished third floor of the building.

Jennifer decided not to comm George for a sit rep. This one simple decision was a victory of sorts. It paired nicely with the decision to shed her suit. The two decisions linked together pulled her anxiety down a notch.

Moving, I have to keep moving, to keep my mind clear from my own toxic thoughts.

Jennifer jogged quickly out into the alley behind the building pulling in lungfuls of air as her legs began to burn softly with each stride. A quick left at the end of the alley put her on the sidewalk heading in the direction of *Rumors*. This late at night the streets were deserted.

At the stop crossing she unslung her rifle gripping it in both hands, picked up her speed, then darted across the street and down the side alley leading to the back of the pleasure club. She kept her mind clear of George, of Ochula, of Jenny, letting her instincts guide her pumping legs down the alley juking a left that would take her to the emergency exit.

Jennifer lurched to a halt in front of a razor-wired-topped dura chain-link fence. The door to the fence had an electro lock with a small scan pad. The entire alley behind the pleasure club was protected by this fifteen-foot-high security fence—which included two ferocious looking Dober dogs forty feet away.

Jennifer saw both animals turn when she came to a halt at the fence line. The scattered glow from a yellow street lamp overhead cast shimmering waves of light off the sleek coats of the brown and black guard dogs. Their lean muscles and broad chests tensed as each dog pushed off with their front legs picking up speed to attack the intruder.

Jennifer snagged the laser blade from her bum bag snicking it on and pressed the electric épée to the lock short circuiting it; the lock clicked open. The two sprinting hounds lunged through the air as the gate opened, sailing through it and missing their target altogether. Jennifer stepped through the open door and closed it, shaking her head at the dogs now on the other side of the fence.

"You guys better work on that," she commented. The dogs were jumping up-and-down barking angrily at her.

Jennifer used the bum bag belt to secure the gate closed. She stuffed the few items from the bag into her blue trouser pockets including the L blade.

Both hands around the rifle, she jogged the hundred or so feet to the emergency exit to *Rumors*. She stopped when the clank of metal behind her startled her. Jennifer wheeled around to find George standing behind her having just landed on the ground in his dura suit. His visor flipped up.

"I cut the feed on my sub-vocal mic when Laura went dark—"

—Just then the heavy metal exit door slammed open clipping the back of Jennifer's head and ass as it flung open. Jennifer pitched forward a half-step blinking and stunned.

George used the servos in his arm to swat Jennifer out of the path of the laser bolt headed for the back of her head. The white bolt tunneled into his left eye instead, drilling deep into his skull, hammering his body backwards to the ground.

Jennifer tried to ignore the danger behind her, woozily resigned to let fate take its course, then scrambled over to George, going down on one knee to look in his uninjured eye.

George was still alive. His mouth opened.

"Thank you for today, Jennifer," he whispered hoarsely, then died right there in the dirty alley.

The volcano of anger intensifying inside Jennifer's sore head blotted out most of the lingering anxiety she felt. A moment of clarity enveloped her instead. Staring into the lifeless open eye the man that had just saved her life, and even thanked her for it, let her accept her own frailties as minor compared to *this*.

A venomous, sneering voice behind Jennifer ordered.

"Stand up!"

Jennifer continued to search George's face hopefully for any signs of life. The weight of her guilt was so heavy she couldn't have pulled herself standing if she wanted to. That was done for her, very roughly.

Hook Nose grabbed her by the back of the hair and lifted. The tactic jerked Jennifer's neck taught lifting her body standing and popping off the sub-vocal mic from her throat. The grip tightened, yanking her hard around, propelling Jennifer in through the open door. The hard jerk pulled the earbud loose too. The little device tumbled to the ground.

The clip to the head slowed Jennifer's reflexes. She wasn't fast enough to aim and fire her weapon as it was wrenched from her grasp by Short Guy.

Hook Nose would not let go of Jennifer's hair, forcing her in staggered pushes down the narrow hall into the second open pleasure room pocket door. He threw her head first into the empty room. By instinct, Jennifer's arms extended as the floor came up fast. No sooner than she caught her weight from a disastrous head-first impact, her pockets were searched and emptied. The door slid closed behind her.

Jennifer grunted herself standing but couldn't decide if she wanted to throw up, scream, or shrivel into a ball and cry. This whole mission dirt-side had unravelled ferociously. She was clear-headed enough to shoulder the blame for leaving Krachy a widower. That in itself was bad enough, but Jennifer had taken a good man with her in George Balliet—not to mention Jenny. Maybe soon, even Laura.

What a shitty Privateer Captain I am, she concluded in tragic self pity.

I should have stayed unemployed.

The door moved aside.

Standing between his two goons was the Prime Minister of Beltina, Lad Blanconales. Blanconales was a handsome, thin, fifty-something man with tan skin and arms crossed confidently peering at his captive behind penetrating gray eyes.

To Jennifer's surprise, he said nothing.

The PM's head turned to Short Guy on his right and nodded once.

Short Guy moved out of sight then returned not ten seconds later with a scared-looking muscular woman with a ripped half-shirt exposing her breasts. Laura Measures was flung roughly into Jennifer's room. Jennifer managed to catch her by the shoulders before she fell. Both of Laura's arms were cinched tightly behind her back.

Short Guy disappeared again then was back fast holding what looked like a foldable chair of some sort.

Blanconales spoke for the first time.

"I'm going to send you two somewhere where you can't get in my way ever again."

Jennifer wrapped an arm around Laura, and in that moment of comforting, Laura looked into Jennifer's eyes and realized what Jennifer had promised earlier that day had, in fact, come to pass.

Laura trusted Jennifer now, just like Jennifer said she would.

The two women didn't really know how they were going to die, but they knew that they were destined to do it together.

Jennifer searched Laura's scared face but could not open her mouth to tell her what had happened to Jenny. That was a dagger that Jennifer would not insert into this dying woman's heart.

No way.

Instead, Jennifer lifted her thinning lips into a sad smile. Fighting past the pain between her ears she said warmly, "I told you, didn't I?"

Laura knew what she meant and seemed to accept her last few moments being comforted by this woman holding her close.

Hook Nose barked.

"Step. The fuck. Back!"

The two woman did what they were told. The laser pistol aimed their way.

Short Guy moved into the room and set the foldable *"chair?"* on the floor on the right side of the room against the base of the wall. The other wall and back of the room formed an L-shaped low couch. He thumbed a switch on one of the four round short legs of the device.

The four legs opened upward. Each leg was telescoping, growing longer and longer as the self-guiding polls elongated pulling with it a thin, sheen, gray sheath as it opened lengthening more. The thin substance snapped taught with a rush of discernible force, like a boat sail pulling tight against the wind. The four thin support tubes framed the seven-foot-high, three-foot-wide facade. Protruding from the right pole, about three feet up the rigid shaft, was a numeric key pad with a red LED light blinking on it.

By instinct, Jennifer's body inched a fraction toward the device—

"—Stay back!" Hook Nose yelled, tensing his grip on the L pistol.

Short Guy touched a key on the numeric pad. The red light turned green. He pecked in a code. The dull shimmering gray veneer ignited into a white flash of brilliance as the portable Coupling Gate switched on with a low hum.

The brightness tunneled through Jennifer's vision assaulting her queasy head.

Both women took in a breath realizing *they* were going to be thrust through the bright light into the depths of *who-knew-where*.

Jennifer pulled Laura closer staring painfully at the same type gate she'd seen at the holding site earlier that evening.

The three men had their evil grins plastered on the helpless women and missed what happened in the middle of the gate.

Laura was looking into Jennifer's eyes and missed it too. Jennifer saw it materialize first.

The dark, small, round tip of the metal barrel lunged from the stark white light growing in length fast. A hand on the underside of the flechette rifle held the forestock; the next hand that quickly materialized held the rifle's grip and trigger. By then, the three men's smiles faded as they too turned their heads sideways at the person charging fast through the gate pointing the weapon directly at them.

Before Lad Blanconale's eyes could widen in fear, the first dart exploded through his chest. The second and third darts drilled each guard at chest level. All three bodies cascaded to the floor one after the other—dead.

Ochula Kozlov's trailing leg completed its journey through the Coupling Gate. His menacing stare pinned the three lifeless men to the floor.

TWENTY

Ochula's mouth was shouting at Jennifer but she couldn't process the sound. And it wasn't because the flechette rifle had just discharged three quick *thift-thift-thifts* in the small room. Jennifer's head was throbbing from the sharp clip she took when the exit door opened.

Gradually, the urgency in Ochula's voice registered in her ears when Laura shouldered her roughly several times to gain her stunned attention. The next strong shove by the body-builder thrust her back into the reality of the moment.

"Take this and untie Laura! Hurry!" Ochula spat, handing Jennifer a laser blade. He had to push it into her hand.

Laura saw Jennifer's fingers finally grip the L blade, all the while anxiously darting her eyes from the blade to Ochula, to the blade, to Ochula, to the blade, to Ochula, countless times in a fidgety feverous impatience that was growing a life of its own.

Ochula turned to the still gleaming Coupling Gate and reached down tapping the keypad.

Laura turned her back to Jennifer presenting her bound wrists so that the tie wrap could be cut. She thrust her cinched wrists up-and-down a bunch of times trying to hurry Jennifer along. Laura's jittery movements kept urging Jennifer to help, her eyes never leaving the back of Ochula's head.

Jennifer finally tightened her grasp on the laser blade, and as carefully as her pulsating head would allow, nicked the thin plasti tie wrap around Laura's wrists trying not to injure her in the process.

Free from her bonds, Laura shot her strong arms from behind her back just as Ochula finished punching at the keypad and turned. She lept at Ochula pulling him against her in a jarring high-octane gratitude fueled embrace.

Laura let go and pushed back awkwardly.

"THANK YOU!! She gasped.

Ochula looked past Laura at Jennifer.

Jennifer's eyes locked onto his. Her face registered that, hammering head or not, she WAS still alive too! Without thinking, Jennifer shoved Laura out of the way so she could get at Ochula to perform a proper thank you of her own.

Not able to find the right way to stop Jennifer's lunge, Ochula simply lifted the flechette rifle up to cross check Jennifer in the sternum. Jenifer's long arms tried to hug him too, but Ochula pushed harder careful not to hurt his friend.

There's no time for this! Ochula's face contorted urgently.

"Stop! You're welcome!" Ochula's eyes landed on Laura's for a brief instant before returning to Jennifer's. "Both of you. We have to get moving!"

Jennifer slurred.

"You'd bwetter let me hug woo later, Ochula!" Jennifer backed away. She looked at Laura.

"Laurwa, can you go next door, the next woom, wherever Blanconales and his thugs stashed my stuff? If you swee a vial of pills I need 'em bad." Jennifer's speech kept deteriorating.

Laura brushed past her fast and cut the corner out into the hall disappearing.

Ochula bent down grabbing Hook Nose's ankles. He looked back at Jennifer behind him.

"Can you help me with this?"

Jennifer nodded absently. The up-and-down motion of her head blurring her vision.

"Shuwer," she prattled by reflex.

After hearing Jennifer mispronounce the simple word "sure," Ochula figured he'd better take Hook Nose's head and shoulders. He scrambled to the dead man's head, looped his hands through his armpits, and lifted as Jennifer made a somewhat helpful grunt lifting the legs of the corpse as best she could.

Ochula motioned with his head at the gate, and the two of them swung the awkward body to-and-fro a few times as Ochula counted, "One…two…three!" On three, they tossed Hook Nose in through the light to *somewhere-land*, his body ingested by the shimmering light—*whoosh*.

Jennifer's head spasmed when her eyes were pierced by the bright light. She stumbled backwards catching herself with outstretched hands as she crashed down onto the soft low couch against the wall.

Laura pulled herself around the door jamb stopping in front of Jennifer. Jennifer looked up trying to focus.

"Here."

Laura already had two pills in her palm. When Jennifer didn't grab them, Laura snatched them up and pushed them between Jennifer's lips. Jennifer tried to swallow, but couldn't do it. No saliva. Her neck strained starting to retch.

An instant later Laura bent down, clamped both hands on Jennifer's ears, pushed her open mouth onto Jennifer's, and gushed a mouthful of her own spit into Jennifer's throat.

Jennifer swallowed breathing through her nostrils. The pills slid down aided by the lubrication.

Laura released her, but before backing away, she crammed Jennifer's pockets with the vial, along with the laser blade and laser pistol shoved into a front pocket. Laura fumbled with the last small, short round item she'd found next door, and it fell to the floor at Jennifer's feet. Jennifer didn't even notice. She just absent-mindedly took stock of her inventory touching each pocket in turn.

Ochula, off to one side tapping a foot, looked at Laura.

"Little help?" His eyes motioned to the dead prime minister.

Laura blinked then bent down by Blanconales pulling him up into her muscular arms, took a step at the Coupling Gate, then looked at Ochula.

"Yeah, toss him through," Ochula instructed.

Laura did. Almost before the brilliance swallowed the body, Laura turned to grab Short Guy. She picked him up and threw him through too.

Blink—gone.

Laura turned to Ochula.

Ochula knew what needed to be done next. He had a plan for everything.

"Laura, I can't be seen. My part in this can never be revealed. It'll start another war. Any minute people are going to come down the hallway wondering what's happening back here. That means you're going to have to stay here to promote the charade."

When Laura's eyes cinched Ochula explained further.

"You're gonna have to make it look like Blanconales and his guards had their way with you then cast you aside before they left out the back door. I know it's thin, but I just sent him and his buddies someplace where they'll never be found."

He looked out into the hallway, at the dark hallway wall, then back at Laura.

"The blood spray is barely noticeable even with all the bright light. Once the gate shuts down they may not even notice it." His eyes landed on the floor. "The spot where they fell isn't that bad either. The carpet's jet black."

Laura nodded in understanding, then both she and Ochula looked over at Jennifer seated on the low couch.

Laura asked.

"What about Jennifer? She coming with you through the gate?"

Ochula's forehead rippled and he shook his head.

"No. She can't come with me to the holding site. That's where I just came from. I programmed the holding site gate to transport me here. Someone has to remove this gate so there's no evidence."

Ochula took two steps stopping in front of Jennifer crouching down in front of her downturned face. He grabbed her hands in his. Jennifer looked at him nauseously.

"Jen, can you grab the gate after I go through it? I'll come and pick you up in George's air car. Get as far away as you can. I'll find you. Use these." Ochula pulled out another set of sub-vocal mic and earbud gently placing the mic on her throat and the bud in an ear. Then Ochula stood looking questioningly at Laura.

Both their faces asked the same thing: *Where's George?*

Ochula turned back to Jennifer.

"Where's George?"

Jennifer heard George's name, her eyes growing wet.

Jennifer mumbled.

"Georwge died saving my life."

Ochula's immalleable determination to finish this mission pushed past his shock and sorrow.

"Where is he?"

"Out back in the alley," Jennifer managed without a slur.

"We can use that." He turned to Laura.

"Laura, you play injured and hurt. Take a few minutes to come around after the staff rouse you awake. They'll find George and pin the PM's disappearance on him. At least long enough for me to get off-planet. You see where I'm headed with this? His body is sterile. He and I made sure there were no identifying items on either of us before we started tonight. The investigation that will start will be focused on him. George was an arms dealer."

Laura would follow Ochula to the ends of the universe after just saving her life. Since she never really liked George in the first place, his death was not the burden it was for Jennifer. She nodded.

"I understand."

Ochula reached in his trouser pocket and pulled out a yellow tab that he palmed then gave to Laura.

"Make sure Jennifer takes this Zofran pill. Help her."

Laura plucked it from his hand and without hesitation stepped over to Jennifer pushing the pill into her mouth with two fingers.

Jennifer absently swallowed several times, barely able to get it to go down.

By the time Jennifer swallowed and Laura turned around, Ochula was not in the room any longer.

It was up to Laura now. Up to her to keep this whole night from unravelling AND to keep herself from being blamed for a nonexistent prime minister. Not only did Laura trust Jennifer, she also wanted her to escape. The fact that George died saving Jennifer wrenched some compassion deep down inside Laura from its locked cage.

There was just one huge problem Laura realized staring at the luminous Coupling Gate.

How the hell do I shut it off?

Before the thought found purchase, the electric discharge of the gate cracked like a whip deactivating itself. The glimmering brilliance snapped off, the tufted sheath of the taught fabric opaque gray now, inactive and inert. Then the telescoping leg frames began retracting into themselves pulling the rectangular structure into a compact bundle on the floor.

Ochula had programmed the device to deactivate once he went through.

Laura helped Jennifer stand. On her feet Jennifer took in several nose fulls of air blowing out the breaths through parted lips.

I only have to hold it together for a little while longer, she concluded. She looked at Laura.

Laura pulled her by the arm toward the door. Jennifer shuffled her feet letting herself be led out of the room. Before Jennifer made the right down the hall to the exit door, Laura bent down scooping up the gate and tucked it under Jennifer's armpit. By reflex Jennifer tensed her arm around it making the right turn out of the room.

Laura started to follow Jennifer to make sure she left then glanced back into the pleasure room to see if she'd missed anything. There, in front of the low couch, was the thin round canister. Laura lurched over toward the couch picking it up. She hurried out of the room catching up with Jennifer just as she left out the exit door. Laura shoved the item into the waist band of Jennifer's trousers at the base of her back.

Jennifer's concentration placing one foot in front of the other negated any feeling of Laura slipping the canister into her pants. Her only concern at the moment was the weight under her arm and trying not to look at George's sprawled body in the alley. Then the loud barking dogs added to her workload. Jennifer thought she heard the heavy metal exit door shut behind her as she made her way to the fence with the jumping, snarling dogs on the other side.

Jennifer pulled out the laser pistol, glanced down at her hand to make sure it was gripped properly, then aimed through the fence. She hesitated unsure if she should fire or not.

What am I waiting for?

Her sickness slackening, she remembered now, then reached down with her other hand to switch the weapon to NL. Non-Lethal mode would only stun, not kill.

Zint! Zint!

The tight white bolts plowed into each dog's broad chest in turn toppling them over with a thud.

Jennifer pushed the LP into a pocket before clumsily undoing the bum bag belt with one hand to let herself out through the gate door.

Out the door she took measured steps cutting right into the stop crossing swinging her free arm to aid her jello legs forward across the street and up the sidewalk as fast as possible, which in actuality was not very fast at all.

More distance started to put *Rumors* behind Jennifer. After ten lung-huffing minutes her journey became less like purgatory and more like a dream. She didn't care that she was lost in the back alleys of Sommerville; she was just thrilled that her intense nausea was finally ebbing.

She looked right, left, then there, up ahead a narrow alley called her name. Almost stumbling in through the mouth of the back street, Jennifer outstretched a hand to catch her balance. She padded fifteen or twenty fast, short, urgent steps to get out of the view from the cross street, shuffling around the far side of a large trash dumpster. She sagged, dropping slowly to the dirty pavement next to the tattered waste bin. Her butt impacted lightly, the Coupling Gate slid from under her arm, then she pulled her legs toward her chest catching her breath.

Let the pills do their job, Jennifer urged silently.

Fifteen minutes later the world was almost Jennifer's oyster.

How can drugs be this effective?

When she tried to stand up, Jennifer realized something could be about to scupper her best laid plans—her still queasy head. Breathing hard from the nixed effort, she eased herself sitting again.

I should know by now that true wellness comes with a rider full of divaish demands.

Plan B: Teamwork makes the dream work...

"Ochula?" Jennifer whispered. "Ochula?"

When static filled her ear instead of her friend's response, Jennifer decided to wait before trying again.

Scratching noises above her in the dim alley pulled her eyes up but she couldn't spot the source. There the sounds were again. She was sure of it.

Jennifer was a confident person by nature and not easily shaken. Having just lived through two imminent life-enders enhanced her bravado that much more.

What else can happen that already hasn't? She surmised.

When the five insect-like creatures scurried down the wall of the building in front of her in a blurring flash of movement,

Jennifer realized that something else sure can happen that already hasn't.

And this is it.

Jennifer Bane froze with knowledge and fear, knowledge that the five Insect Aliens in front of her were a part of the rogue faction of their race here to kill her. Fear that her pockets were being emptied so fast that she had zero chance—none—to pull out her LP and defend herself.

The search and removal by the closest IA reminded Jennifer of the order in which she took inventory of her pockets right after Laura filled them back at *Rumors*.

It was at that moment that she realized that the IAs had been reading her thoughts all evening—just like George had said they were ever since coming dirt-side.

Jennifer also understood why the vial of pills in her pocket were not confiscated along with the L blade and laser pistol—the pills were not a threat to the IAs.

Damn if I'm going to die lying down, she huffed in defiance to herself then started to stand up. As she did, the canister Jennifer was not even aware she had scraped against the brick wall behind her nudging it against the small of her back.

In that fleeting instant of realization Jennifer acted.

Her legs tensed pushing up, her left arm extended upward the fingers inserting into the small gap between the top of the dumpster and the lid pulling hard, her right hand reaching around behind her back grabbing the incendiary boomer activating it.

All five IAs processed Jennifer's thought at the exact same time: ATTACK!

By then Jennifer had already leapt up under the lid of the dumpster yanking herself inside with her left hand aided by a desperate push with her long legs. The boomer flicked free from her right hand cascading end-over-end through the air toward the IAs. Before it hit the ground it detonated.

Jennifer's right hand disappeared under the closing lid just as the self-igniting white phosphorus and thermite explosion lit up the alley in a blinding flash of incendiary force. The shockwave pushed the sticky death blaze against the fronts of all five IAs in a high-temperature reaction that was hot enough to melt metal—which it did. Jennifer's confiscated LP wilted and drooped instantly along with the leg of the IA holding it.

The searing heat engulfing the five-member death squad slammed the assassins backwards to the pavement. The hard carapaces of the dying bugs crackled and popped under the intensive heat of the sustained energy sources.

The firestorm wave smacked itself against the front and side of the dumpster so hard the large bin quaked. The gluey inferno coated scattered portions of the dumpster's surface, burning hotly, assaulting the metal.

Inside her life-saving container, Jennifer's face pressed against the thrown out food stuffs and garbage lining the bin's floor. Instead of lifting her nose from the foul stench filling it, she wrapped her arms around the slimy garbage, pulling it to her chest like Krachy sleeping next to her in bed.

The sides of the dumpster closest to the epicenter began to deform and melt. Just then the AI sensor inside the auto-bin sensed the added weight of Jennifer's body. The automated trash receptacle registered the increase as *full*, then the bottom gave way, opening down the center of the floor, to deposit the day's trash onto the conveyor belt trash removal system underneath the alley.

Jennifer and the viscous trash free fell the eight feet impacting the moving conveyor belt with a splat. All the air was pushed from her lungs.

"Jennifer? Jennifer? Jennifer, you there?" Slowly the words began to amplify inside her head.

Jennifer lifted her face from the trash pillow watching the narrow walls of the city's automated trash removal tunnel move her towards Sommerville's waste collection site.

Before Jennifer could respond to the comm, the conveyor belt spit her out the tunnel opening onto the top of a growing mound of city refuse. She managed to catch her weight with outstretched hands, but not before what seemed like another fifty pounds of glop poured down on top of her from the ejecting belt.

The increased weight of more garbage being deposited on top of Jennifer stopped. She clawed her way up and through the avalanche of filth her face finally breaching the top of the large mound.

"I'm at the city's solid waist collection site, Ochula. Come get me!" She yelled enthusiastically. The smile on her face while she grunted and pulled her putrid body atop the trash heap grew wider as she became less and less submerged.

Finally sitting atop the peak, Jennifer watched Ochula jerk the air car to a hard stop at the base of the immense trash pile.

Ochula sprang from the air car looking up at Jennifer frantically.

"Holy shit, I thought you were dead!" He yelped.

"No way! It'll take a lot more than this to make me some smelly-assed *Fatal Delivery*."

Jennifer Bane's face could not have held a wider grin.

EPILOGUE

"This gunge is starting to harden on me," an absolutely repugnant Jennifer Bane commented from the passenger seat of the air car. The adrenaline rush from her escape had cleared her head for the most part. Unfortunately, her nose worked okay too.

"We're almost there," Ochula assured, guiding the vehicle around a corner getting closer to Darla's spillway less than a half mile away. It was just coming up on 3am.

Even with all the windows in the air car down, the stench was overwhelming. The moving air was also making the crud-batter coating on Jennifer's body coagulate.

Jennifer had to force her face to turn toward her friend. The slime encapsulating her shoulders and neck had started to solidify.

"So you gonna let me thank you for saving my life back at *Rumors*?"

Ochula's eyelids arched flicking a reluctant look her way.

"What? You mean now?"

Jennifer lurched her stinky body toward his. A small jagged slab of slurry on her chest pulled free with the movement landing in her lap with a *squish*.

Inches away from his ear Jennifer coaxed.

"Turn this way, Ochula. Time for that hug."

Head still straight ahead.

"Is this something you feel strongly about, Jen?" Ochula asked incredulously, clearly not wanting to hug Stank Face.

"I may let you slide on the hug if you explain your Come-Through-The-Coupling-Gate-Miraculous-Timing thing." Jennifer pulled her rigid body back into her seat with considerable effort. Her jittery eyes looked down at the cocoon forming around her and added quickly, "Better hurry though. I'm turning into a statue over here."

Ochula spotted the spillway crest at Darla's place up ahead, pushed at the controls to guide the air car over the apex, then brought the air car to an angled stop under the *Mural Bridge*. No one was around at the moment.

He was eager to comply with the *gate* request if it would cancel out the *hug* request.

Ochula turned in his seat looking at Jennifer fighting the urge to pinch his nose closed.

"George gave me the geo-location of *Rumors* after he dropped Laura off. I punched those coordinates into the Coupling Gate at the holding site. The holding site gate scanned for a coordinate lock. Once the gate at *Rumors* switched on, I stepped through and—"

"—saved our lives." Jennifer finished his sentence. "You knew Blanconales had a portable gate." It wasn't a question.

Ochula shrugged.

"It only made sense after what we discovered at the holding site."

"And you used me as a means to an end." Again, not a question.

"You did great though, didn't you?" He tried to distance himself from using his friend so dangerously.

Ochula's look turned sad.

"I'm sorry I wasn't there to help George. I'm also sorry about—"

Jennifer's crusty brows lifted.

"—Jenny?"

"Yes, Jenny. I'm truly sorry, Jen."

Jennifer's face was neutral, accepting it all now. However...

"Can you look in the back seat for me? I'm afraid to." Jennifer wasn't sure she could take seeing Jenny's body back there. Besides, Glue Girl couldn't turn to look behind her if she wanted to.

Ochula didn't look in the back seat, but mentioned instead, "I gently placed Jenny's body in the boot before coming to pick you up."

Jennifer swallowed.

"What am I going to tell Laura?"

Ochula shook his head firmly.

"YOU aren't going to tell her anything. It was MY fault. I'll tell her."

Jennifer feigned shaking her head in disbelief. She wanted to shake it, but it was frozen stiff.

"I can't make you do that, Ochula. You've already done enough for me, for this planet. You have to let me shoulder some of the load."

"I didn't say I was going to tell Laura in person, Jennifer. I have to get off-planet fast or everything we did will fall apart. If I'm identified, the war you and I helped stop years ago will start up all over again."

"What about Laura?" Jennifer persisted.

"Darla is going to do it for me."

Jennifer gawked. Then finally her mouth opened.

"Does Darla know about this?"

"No. Asking her to do it can be your way of shouldering some of the load. You know my tight beam trans code. Give it to Darla so that when Laura wants an explanation, she can comm me to get one."

Jennifer knew this was the best Ochula could offer given the circumstances. She also knew what he didn't say: *I'm going to have to tell Darla about George.* She had quite the burden after all it seemed…and was glad about that. Of course she was glad about anything right now.

Alive and gunky was so much better than dead and dirt free.

Ochula started to fidget in his seat. And it wasn't because of Jennifer's reek. He had to leave. The chrono was ticking behind his concerned eyes.

Jennifer saw it.

"My attack shuttle is at the Sommerville spaceport. Use it to get off-planet. You have my hand comp. The access codes are in it. I know you can't go to the holding site again to use the Coupling Gate. You've risked going there twice tonight. I had to destroy the portable gate from *Rumors* to…" Jennifer stammered picturing the death squad she deep-fried in the alley, "to—never mind. Once you're safe, have Ian come dirtside and pick me up. I can make my way to Sommerville's spaceport this evening. I'll meet him there. Everyone, or every being, that's a threat," Jennifer eyes strengthened. "…is gone."

"You gonna introduce me, Jennifer, or what?" A woman's voice asked through the passenger window.

Jennifer recognized Darla's voice. Before she could respond, Ochula came around the front of the air car meeting Darla in front of the hood. Darla was short standing next to him glancing Jennifer's way several times as they talked. The headlamps were bright against their bodies.

Ochula came back to the driver side, bent down and kneeled on the seat, then looked past Jennifer at Darla. The passenger door was already open.

"On three, Darla…" Ochula placed his outstretched hands on Jennifer's gooey shoulder. Darla nodded, ready to help.

"One..two..three," Ochula pushed, Darla pulled, and Jennifer slurped out of the seat with a lurch sideways, Darla guiding her to a landing next to the air car with a *sput*.

Jennifer's eyes focused.

The headlamps illuminated the far side of the spillway under the bridge. The mural was gone. The only thing left was flowing, dripping, rivulets of color where the large curved underside of the bridge had been wet down and scrubbed of all evidence.

Jennifer grunted when Darla pulled her sitting with a firm tug.

Jennifer heard the boot to the air car open then a few moments later close. She was thankful she couldn't see Jenny's body that Ochula had placed on the ground. Ochula climbed back behind the controls and the air car hummed to life, the auto-doors closing. It glided in a turn heading up and out of the spillway the way it came.

Darla sat down in front of Jennifer locking eyes making it a point not to glance behind her at the body.

"I'm the reason George is dead, Darla," Jennifer whispered.

Darla reached out grabbing Jennifer's squishy hand.

"No, he's the reason you're alive. I was just lucky to have known him at all."

"He saved my life and your planet. There won't be any more abductions."

"I told you all of us were important."

"You were right. ALL of us ARE…"

References:

- The flash mob scene in Darla's spillway inspired by the song Lost In Music. Performed by Sister Sledge. Written and produced by Nile Rodgers and Bernard Edwards. Released by Cotillion Records and Atlantic Records in 1979.